D0925006

A Special Thanks To My Sponsors
Who Made This Book Possible—

Willamette Industries
Lebanon, Oregon

Stone Forest Industries
Springfield, Oregon

Starfire Lumber Co.
Cottage Grove, Oregon

Reed's Fuel & Trucking
Springfield, Oregon

Nordic Veneer
Roseburg, Oregon

Surcamp Logging
Springfield, Oregon

Pioneer Truck Plaza
Brownville, Oregon

Vintage Inn Restaurant
Cottage Grove, Oregon

Far West Truck Center
Eugene, Oregon

Dee's Thriftway Market
Cottage Grove, Oregon

THE
GHOST
OF
PORTERVILLE

THE Ghost OF Porterville

by
Bob Glenn

~~Solm Publishing~~
~~P.O. Box 588~~
Cottage Grove, Oregon
1661 N. Pacific Hwy. #20
Cottage Grove, OR 97424

Copyright 1993 by Bob Glenn
All rights reserved.
No part of this book/material may be reproduced or utilized
in any form or by any means, electronic or mechanical,
without written permission from the copyright owner.

International Standard Book Number: 0-9639368-0-8

Library of Congress Cataloging-in-Publication Data
(Prepared by Quality Books Inc.)

Glenn, Bob.
    The ghost of Porterville / by Bob Glenn.
    p. cm.
    ISBN 0-9639368-0-8

    I. Title.

PS3557.L455G56 1993   813'.54
                                    QBI93-22200

Available From:
Soln Publishing
PO Box 588
Cottage Grove, OR 97424

First Edition

Cover Design and Illustrations by
Jim Carpenter

Production and Printing by
WESTERN PRINTERS
Eugene, Oregon

To my wife Joan

Acknowledgements

*With gratitude to my friends
and all the people
who have read my manuscript
and who have encouraged me
along the way with this book.
And special thanks to Jeralee Swearingen
who did my typing and who encouraged me to
keep going to completion.*

Chapter 1

The sun was just coming up over the far mountain range, as Merle and Bob slipped the small fishing boat into the water. Neither man saying anything, each knew exactly what the other was doing—they had done this so many times before.

Bob held the boat into the dock, while Merle drove the pickup and empty trailer up and parked it in the almost empty parking lot. "Come on, Gus!" Merle said. "Let's go fishing." The little dog jumped from the seat to the ground, and headed for the boat. When Merle arrived at the boat, Bob had the little motor running to warm up and was rigging up his fishing pole. Gus had made his way to the front and was lying down in his usual place on top of the life preservers. Merle stepped aboard and took his seat, back by the motor.

"Okay, Bob! Turn it loose." Merle turned the throttle and they moved away from the dock.

"Should be some fish over by the point," Bob exclaimed. "We knocked them dead over there last time, remember?"

Merle turned the boat a little to the left and headed for the peninsula on the far side of the lake. About three hundred yards away, Merle slowed the boat to a trawling speed so they could drop their combination of lures, lines and hooks over the side.

Walt pulled his jeep to the viewpoint parking area, got out and walked out on the point. What he saw was almost hypnotic. The lake was like a mirror. The far mountains reflecting in the glassy water were an exact duplicate. A light fog outlined the shoreline and a small silver boat slipping through the water, down by the point.

"Damn!" he said, "I should've set my alarm. One thing about these two, if you're not here, they go right on without you. Course, I didn't tell them for sure that I was going. I'll drive on down to the peninsula and see if I can get their attention."

Merle, Walt, and Bob were as compatible as three men could possibly be. They worked at the mill together and after they had completed raising their children, they played together.

Their wives and children also had a close relationship. Because of the friendship of the three men, these families were thrown together as one large family.

In the summer months, many weekends were spent at Walt's little cabin at the beach. There they dug clams, did their crabbing off the small pier, flew homemade kites, and sat around a campfire on the beach until late at night, singing and telling stories.

When they stayed at home on weekends, there

was always a picnic, barbecue, and baseball game which involved some of the kids. Yes, this was a happy time for these families and they built bonds that would last a lifetime.

Merle steered the boat past the point and started a long sweeping turn to make another pass just a little farther out. Bob was leaning back in his seat, hat drawn over his eyes. "Ya know, Merle!" Bob said, as if he was sleep talking, "six more years and we can do this every day if we want to, yah! That would be an easy way for us both to get divorced, don't you think?"

"I think you're probably right there," Merle replied. "Hey! Look over there. Old Walt did get out of bed after all. Pull in your line. No, better yet, let's act like we didn't see him for a while."

Walt stood on the bank, waving his hat and shouting. The two men in the boat didn't look up or seem to notice. He murmured, "These guys are not only blind, but can't hear either."

"We better go get him," Merle said. "Gus has given us away." Gus had stood up and was looking at Walt on the bank, his stub of a tail was wagging in happy recognition.

"Mona finally get off your shirt tail?" Merle asked as the boat slid up to the rock where Walt was standing.

"Nah!" Walt said, "I thought I'd better get out here. You guys never catch anything unless I'm along. Just couldn't see you wasting a whole day."

"Hell, Merle! Look at all that stuff. He doesn't come to fish, just eat!" observed Bob as he held the boat to the rock while Walt loaded his pole, tackle box, food box and two large bottles of coffee.

"Well, at least we can fish a while," Walt said. "We won't have to leave at noon, just because you two are hungry."

And so it is in Green Valley on a Saturday morning. An old boat, a little yellow dog, and three good friends fishing, laughing, and chattering the day away.

Gus lay on the front porch looking down the lane at the mailbox thinking it was time to walk down there to meet his master. He was a small Golden Cocker about two years old, give or take a couple of months.

It was the middle of January. Dark clouds and mist engulfed the whole valley. Green Valley was thirty miles long, two to three miles wide, with tall fir trees and lush, green pastures—meadows with many types of flowers and shrubs.

In the summer the valley was one of the most beautiful places on earth, but in the winter months the clouds, fog and drizzle made it downright miserable for work or play. That's the way it was on this day. Gus got up and slowly walked down the lane knowing soon that the old blue pickup would pull in the drive and stop at the mailbox. His friend and

owner would get out, leave the door open while he retrieved the mail and paper. Gus would jump in for the ride back to the house. This had been his ritual as long as he could remember. It was a special time for Gus, a time to have his ears rubbed and to hear the gentle words that accompanied the soft strokes on the ride back to the house.

Gus waited. Suddenly, looking down the empty road, he could hear the old truck. The muffler had worn out several months ago and could be heard before it rounded the curve. The pickup pulled into the drive, stopped at the mailbox where Merle's first words were always the same, "Gus, if your feet are wet, don't get on the seat." Gus would jump in on the floor boards, run to the far side, jump on the seat and before Merle could get the door closed, inch his way across the seat and lay his head on Merle's leg for his daily dose of affection.

Merle was a man six feet two in his stocking feet. He was large in his shoulders and chest. The years had put a little weight on his mid-section. At fifty-five he was a fine specimen of a man with sandy colored hair, grey at the temples, and laugh wrinkles around his pale blue eyes and a mouth that seemed to always smile. He looked and acted like a man that could carry the world on his shoulders and still smile about it.

Merle stopped his pickup in front of a lean-to woodshed—a simple structure, just good enough to keep the winter's wood supply dry. He got out and sat down on the chopping block to unlace his heavy work boots. The last thing he wanted to do was track mud and dirt in on Em's always clean floor. "Ya know Gus, things are going to be different around here. The mill closed today and I don't have any idea what I'm going to do. You and Mom are going to have a grumpy old man to contend with until I can find another job." As he slipped on his slippers, he looked over the valley before him. Much had changed in the last thirty-one happy years.

He and Emma had left an Iowa dirt farm, owned by Emma's folks. He was a field hand and Emma helped her mom cook for the farm hands. It was a good life, full of hard work, family gatherings and a lot of love for all. Everything was fine until the summer of 1960, a year of poor crops, low prices and non-cooperating bankers. The farm had to be sold to pay off debts and secure the retirement of Emma's mom and dad. "We're going to Oregon," he told Em. "I hear there's work out there for all who want to work." They settled in this little valley in June of '61, went to work at Green Valley Lumber, a mile up the road, and made a small down payment on this house and acreage.

They had twin boys Simon and Peter. (He, Simon Peter, had been Em's favorite disciple in the Bible.) They grew up, seems like overnight, and started their own worlds. Simon was a lawyer in Portland. He had a wife and three little girls—Em's pride and joy. She always wanted a little girl, but the Lord blessed them with just the two boys, that's all. Peter hasn't married yet. He says he wants a girl like Mom and just hasn't found one yet.

The aroma of dinner brought him suddenly awake. "Yes, Gus! It's been a good life here in the valley. One that I wouldn't trade for all the dirt in Iowa." He stood up, picked up an arm load of wood and made his way to the back door.

"Hi, Em! I'm home!"

Merle sat at the kitchen table, looking down the same lane at the same mailbox. He thought to himself, "Things have really changed. The mill closed five years ago. Four years ago Em passed away—had a stroke in the middle of the night and just never woke up. Simon took a job with the State Department in Washington, D.C. shortly after the funeral. Peter doesn't write much now. Haven't had a letter in months. The last of the savings and what I could borrow went for Em's funeral. I wouldn't take help from the boys. Guess I was just too proud. A few odd jobs have kept me going, but now here it is winter, no jobs to be had, spent my last five dollars for dog food for Gus. Things could be worse but I don't exactly know how."

Merle added some wood to the fire and walked to the cupboard to see what was left. "Not much left here, Gus. Let's see, three potatoes, two cans of milk, one half bag of beans and just a little coffee. What in the heck can I make out of that?!"

He reached down and patted Gus on the head. "Well, boy, looks like we'll take the old gun and shoot us a deer. Oh, I know it's not hunting season, but what the heck. If they put me in jail at least there'd be food there."

He reached behind the wood stove, picked up the old rifle, checked the action, wiped it free of dust with a dirty towel, and took the shell box from the drawer. "Huh? Wouldn't ya know it. Just three shells left. I'd better shoot good, boy, if we're going to eat the rest of the winter."

It was lightly raining when Merle and Gus walked up the trail behind the house. "Bet those deer are up in the trees to stay dry. If they aren't, they're dumber than a rock." He had been up this same trail with his rifle, but always in season. "I very seldom shot a deer, really don't care much for the taste. They seem so helpless in the sight of a rifle, but we can't think about things like that. We're too hungry to be soft."

As Merle walked, his eyes swept the meadow under the trees, looking at the trail for tracks. Up around the corner there was an old orchard, must have been a homestead at one time. Late in the fall there were always deer close by, eating the few apples and pears that fell from the old trees.

He and Em came up here a lot to pick fruit for their jams and jellies. Merle did most of the picking, while Em picked wild flowers to decorate the house.

As they approached the meadow, they inched around the brush to see if anything was there, before they were seen. Probably nothing there. Gus would be acting up if there were; being a Spaniel, he would never bark, just his excitement would tell me. As the orchard came into view, sure enough, nothing.

"Well, Gus, the next place to look is up by the waterfall. Years ago I killed a nice four-point up there." They left the orchard and went up a game trail leading into a small side canyon. Rain was falling harder now and the mist and fog were just a few feet over his head. "If we don't see one soon we won't be able to." Suddenly Gus stopped dead still and was looking off the trail toward a grove of thickly bunched fir trees. "There's one," he whispered to Gus as he raised his gun for a shot. He held his breath and squeezed the trigger. The rifle jumped in his hands and the small buck was down. Merle waited a couple of minutes to make sure he wouldn't get up and run. Then slowly they walked toward the spot where the deer fell. They had walked about fifty feet, when the buck struggled to his feet and started up through the bush dragging his hind quarters. "Can't go far, Gus. We'll just follow him till he lies down. Don't want to use any more bullets. Might need them later."

Merle and Gus followed the blood signs as they walked around the dense underbrush. "He can't go far. He's losing a lot of blood. He should fall at any time." The sound of the small waterfall was close now. "He can't go much farther. This is a dead end canyon." The little waterfall was only about one foot wide and dropped seven or eight feet. It was strictly a winter falls. In summer it dried up. "There it is, Gus, but I don't see the buck any place. There's his blood, but no buck." Gus was looking up the cliff. Sure enough, there he was—still struggling. "How in thunder did he get up there?" Merle muttered as he looked at the sheer cliff. Gus sniffed the blood pool then started back down the trail when he saw a faint game trail going off and up to the right. That must be the way. "Come on, Gus. Let's go." The trail led to a small ledge just wide enough to walk on. Slowly, they made their way along the slippery ledge. Rounding an outcropping it widened out to about a thirty foot wide area. Grass and small pools of water were in every low spot on the ledge. "Beautiful spot,

Gus. A good place to hide out if I need to. Those bill collectors get down right nasty."

Around a large boulder that had fallen from the cliff above, lay the little buck, wet with rain and blood, forming a red pool where he was lying. The rain was falling harder now. Merle was looking around for a little protection to do his butchering. He noticed a cut out in the cliff at the far end. "Don't look too big, but I bet it's drier than here." He grabbed the small buck by the horns, carried his rifle with the other, and dragged the deer up to the opening. The overhang was about thirty feet deep. The roof of the cave started about eight feet then tapered back to two or three feet in height. There was sand four or five inches deep on the floor and looked as if it hadn't been disturbed in years.

Over against the far wall was a large pack rat's nest. Plenty of good dry wood. Tearing it apart, Merle proceeded to lay a fire. The dry sticks and dead grass made the fire jump to life, putting out a warming glow bouncing off the cave walls.

Standing there warming his hands and watching the steam come off his pants and jacket, Merle spoke more to himself than to Gus. "Soon as I warm up, I'll skin and cut up this little critter. If I can only make him last till . . . let's see . . . this is Friday the fourteenth and I get my first Social Security check on the third. That's nineteen more days. Don't know if I can make it. Might have to do this again."

Getting out his knife, he walked back to where

the buck was lying to drag him closer to the fire. "Gus! What in the heck are you doing out there? Get in here by the fire and get warm." Gus was just inside the overhang barely out of the rain, looking back at the dark part of the cave. "Come on in and get dry you dummy. You'll be wet again before we get back to the house." Gus did not move or seem to hear anything that Merle said, so Merle walked out and grabbed Gus by the collar. Gus did not want to come, so Merle pulled him, his feet sliding in the soft sand. "Now! Lay there and get warm." When Merle let go of his collar, Gus darted back to the place where he had been lying, looking at the back of the cave, whimpering softly.

"Well, I wonder what's got into that darn fool dog! I wonder if there's something in here that he's afraid of and maybe I should be too. I'd better look this place over a little better." Going to the pile of sticks in the nest, he picked out a long one to use as a torch. He touched it to the fire and soon had a large flame bright enough to light his way. Picking up his rifle, Merle walked off to the left, which was the only dark area of the cave. Sure enough, a smaller cave entrance was running deeper into the mountain. Inching his way along the narrow passage, he spoke to himself. "Wouldn't it be something if I found a vein of gold six feet wide. Just dreaming. Better pay attention. Might be something in there."

The cave made a bend to the right and as he rounded the end of the bend he could see a light, a

bright light. "I'll be damned, another entrance." He quickened his pace. The farther he went, the larger the cave and the brighter the light. . . .

Coming to the entrance, Merle couldn't believe his eyes. There was another valley, a beautiful valley. Tall trees, flowers, rippling waters and large green meadows. There were bees and birds everywhere. Merle stood there amazed and confused. The sun was out. White puff clouds floated across the blue sky. This can't be. This is the fourteenth of January. On the other side of the mountain it's cold and rainy. . . . .

"This is just like summer. I'm going after Gus and show him there's nothing to be afraid of." Back through the tunnel Merle swiftly went, picked Gus up in his arms, and went back through the tunnel, almost at a run—except in the darkest part.

A narrow flower ladened path marked by stones seemed to beckon Merle. So with Gus still in his arms, he walked down the trail absorbing the beauty and the warmth that seemed to be everywhere. Merle's footsteps brought them to a tiny picturesque area where an infant waterfall, of two or three feet in height, dropped into a small clear pool. Merle stood looking at the pool, the mountains, the trees and meadows. "This," he said to Gus, "is going to be our secret place."

Turning and looking behind him, Merle saw a very old, weathered stone bench. "It has been many years since someone has used that to sit on," he thought as he climbed the bank and eased himself down to sit upon it. As he sat there, he put Gus beside him. Gus inched closer and closer, like he always did in the old truck.

He even closed his eyes and seemed to fall asleep.

Suddenly Gus opened his eyes, jumped to the ground and ran up the trail into the cave entrance.

"Well, I guess he's telling me it's time to go. We've got quite a bit of work to do before we can eat."

As he put his hands down on the bench to give himself a boost up, his left hand felt something that didn't feel like stone. Looking down he saw that it was a rolled-up newspaper. "I never noticed that when I sat down," he thought, picking it up and unrolling the paper. "Well, I'll be. The Valley News." Rolling it back up and sticking it in his hip pocket, Merle picked up his rifle and headed back toward the cave entrance.

"It has been quite a day, Gus."

Merle felt good as he cut up some back strap and placed it in the frying pan alongside some newly sliced potatoes.

Chapter 2
The Discovery

After eating his fill of venison and fried potatoes, Merle filled his cup with hot, black coffee and picked up the rolled-up paper. "Seems good to have a paper in the house again." He'd been going without, since his subscription ran out last November. "Yes, sir! I'm going to enjoy every page of this here paper."

The headlines read: "Snow and icy roads make driving hazardous in the valley." Merle read about the many accidents, fallen trees and power outages. After living here all these years, this wasn't really news. It happened almost every year about this time.

As he made his way through article after article, he came to a smaller headline stating: "Someone has the winning ticket for the Oregon lottery jackpot of ten million dollars." The article went on to say the winning numbers were 7-19-20-31-32-40. The lucky winner would receive four hundred sixty-eight thousand dollars a year for the next twenty years, after taxes.

"By golly, Gus, that's more money than an old

man like me could spend in a whole lifetime. No one person should have all that kinda money." He laid that section aside and picked up the comics—Merle was a Beetle Bailey fan. "Best part of the paper," he said aloud. "A person needs to laugh some of the time." As he started through the comics, he suddenly stopped. "This is a Sunday paper and this is only Friday. I'm sure it's only Friday."

Putting down the comics and returning to the front page, Merle saw across the top, "Sunday, January 16, 1993." He jumped up and went hurriedly to his calendar hanging on the far wall. Sure enough, according to it this was Friday the fourteenth day of January. He was sure for he had been marking off the days until he received his first Social Security check.

"Boy! Gus, I don't understand this . . . if I'm right, then these are the numbers for tomorrow's drawing. I'm probably wrong, but everything about today has been kinda odd, like a dream or something."

Slipping on his still damp jacket, Merle called, "Come on, Gus. Let's drive down to Larry Flick's place and see if I can look at their today's paper." Larry lived down the road towards town. He had worked with Merle at the mill until it closed, then he found a job as a janitor at the school. It didn't pay much, but it kept him afloat until he started his Social Security two years ago. Since then he and his wife Cora were doing all right.

It was dark now as Merle drove from the lane out onto the highway. There was a steady rain hitting the windshield and the old wipers were doing the best they could. "I should have replaced those things last year," he thought. "Well, maybe when I get my check I can start buying a few things. Simon has offered to help several times, but I'm just too proud to let him know just how bad it's gotten."

There were no lights on in the house and no car in the carport, Merle noticed as he turned into Larry's driveway. "Oh, hell! We'll just have to come back in the morning. I don't want to waste gas to go any farther." As Merle backed his truck out on the road and started his turn to go back home, he noticed something that almost made his heart stop. His headlights had lit up the mailbox and alongside the box was a newspaper. "The paper's still there. They must have been gone all day," he thought. Driving his truck up alongside the box, he withdrew the paper. By a very dim dome light he read the date on the paper: "Friday, January 14, 1993."

"Son-of-a-gun. I'll be damned," he said aloud as he returned the paper to the mailbox. "Come on, Gus! Let's get home. We've got things to do."

Sitting at the kitchen table looking again and again at the numbers in the paper, Merle suddenly felt old. Hell, he was old. The last five years had turned his hair completely grey, stooped his shoulders and bowed his back.

He sipped the last of the coffee and thought of the many friends that he had made in the years that he'd lived in Porterville—Bill, Bob, Les, Cliff, Wayne, Walt.

Oh, well! Really there's too many to recall all at this moment. But he was sure that many of them were in the same financial straits that he was in.

"We're going to town in the morning, Gus. We'll meet the guys at the coffee shop, see if I can borrow a few bucks to get this thing going. I can't tell them anything, don't want to make a fool of myself. After all, this still could be only a dream."

Merle pulled his pickup into the parking lot of the village cafe. "Gosh, Gus! We haven't been here since before Christmas. I'm a little early, but I'm sure some of the guys will show up."

Merle walked in, exchanging good mornings to several people that he recognized as he made his way to the old familiar table by the window. "None of my friends are here yet!" he thought to himself. "Still a little early yet. Maybe I can build up a little courage for what I need to do."

Linda, a small blond waitress, noticed Merle and was soon there with his water and a mug of hot coffee. "Merle! Where in thunder have you been? We all thought you'd died or went to see your son or something. You haven't been around for a month or so. We were about ready to send a search party out for you."

"Gosh, Linda! I'm so broke that I couldn't afford to come to town. The only reason I'm here now is I knew you'd buy the coffee." Linda chuckled, "I'll buy your coffee any time. By the way, when are you going to marry me? I make enough in tips to keep us both going." They both laughed at that. "We've sure missed you, Merle. The guys will be glad you're back. Here they come now. I'd better get the coffee set up. I don't want a bunch of old men growling at me."

Out the window, Merle saw Bob and Walt drive in, followed by Bill and Jim. The rest will be along. They always are. Bob came charging through the door, Walt close behind. He'd seen Merle's old pickup parked out in front. "Where in the blazes have you been? We've begun to think you didn't like us anymore." "Yah!" Walt said, "I drove out to your place yesterday. Your truck was there, but you were nowhere around."

"I was a little troubled," Merle explained, "so Gus and I took a walk up on the hill. Just trying to sort things out. Sorry I missed you." One by one the rest came in exchanging the rhetoric that happens when one of them is gone for a few days.

They huddled around the table talking about the usual things: the weather, politics, and steelhead fishing down on the river. Merle swallowed his pride and asked the question that he knew he had to ask. "Fellows," he said, "I'm in a real tight spot right now. I need to borrow a little money for a few days. Can any of you help me out?"

All of them spoke at once. You couldn't make out what they were saying. They sounded like a bunch of excited magpies. "Hold it! Hold it!" shouted Bob. Silence settled over the group. "You mean that's why we haven't seen you lately? Because you didn't have any money? How much do you need, Merle? Among all of us we can come up with enough to get you through this." Merle looked down at his coffee feeling a little embarrassed. "If I could get my hands on forty or fifty dollars, I think I could make it through."

Bob reached in his pocket and pulled out a ten dollar bill and laid it on the table. "For all that you've done for me over the years. If you still come up short, let me know. I'll go home and sell the wife," he said, closing with a hardy laugh. Each man reached into his purse and pulled out whatever bills he had and in turn thanked Merle for the many favors of the past.

Bob pushed the pile of money over in front of Merle. "Here it is ole man! But now you'll have to buy the coffee, we're all broke." Merle could hardly hold back the tears as he took the money, stacked it neatly, folded it and put it in his shirt pocket. "What a heck of a bunch of friends you are. I'll see that you get it all back in just a few days."

After the "see ya' laters" and the pats on the backs, they left as they had come—one by one, two by two. Merle sat alone filled with gratitude for these men and the whole world at this moment.

Merle was deep in thought. What if the numbers he picked today were winners? What if this wasn't a mix-up of some sort? What would he do with the money? "I'll get the money first and worry about spending it later," he thought.

On his way home Merle stopped at the little Shop and Go market, picked up a few items that he needed and took his basket to the counter. "How do you play that lottery game?" he asked the clerk. She handed him a slip, pointed to the many squares with numbers. "Black out the numbers you want to play. Give it to me and I'll put it through the machine and it'll print your ticket."

Merle took the small paper from his pocket, carefully marked his numbers, then gave the slip back to the clerk. She put it in her machine and handed him back his ticket. "Good luck!" she said. "I hope it's a winner. That'll be eight dollars and thirty-nine cents for the groceries and the ticket."

He took ten dollars from the money he'd borrowed and paid the clerk. Merle felt good. He had a nervous feeling in his stomach—like he got just before catching a big fish. Later that evening he sat in his overstuffed chair waiting for the numbers to be drawn. Not paying much attention to the existing program, just killing time, lost in his own day dreams.

All that money, what would he do? What would he buy? Suddenly he brought himself back to reality. He didn't have any money. He hadn't won anything yet. Again the thought entered his mind, "What'll I do with the money? My needs are small. I know! It would be nice to help other people, make their lives a little easier. Do something for Porterville—make it a nicer town. Help the elderly. Help the needy. But if I do win, I don't want them to think I'm a free 'hand out,' but I can figure that out later."

Taking the ticket from his pocket, he was leaning forward in his chair, just a couple more minutes and he would know. The commercials were just finishing. Merle was holding the ticket so tightly that his fingers were almost white. Although the house was cool, sweat was beading up on his forehead. The program began. After a short introduction, the announcer began reading the balls as they jumped into place. "The first number is thirty-one. The second is seven. The third is forty. The fourth number is twenty. The fifth number is nineteen and the final number is thirty-two."

Merle jumped form his chair. "It's not a dream! It's not a dream! I've won! I've won!"

By Sunday night, Merle knew what he was going to do and how he was going to make it work. Going through the drawer getting out clean socks and underwear, he looked at the picture of Em on the dresser. "Sure wish you were here, honey. We could do so many things together. All those things that we never had the time or the money for in the past. This money's not going to mean nearly as much without you. Not nearly as much."

Chapter 3
The Plan

Monday morning found Merle, with Gus, headng north on the freeway. He had decided to stop at Spring City and see a lawyer friend of Simon's. Paul and Simon had attended and graduated from the University together and had been best friends for the several years that they were there. Simon would often bring Paul home just to enjoy some of Em's home cooked meals and some fishing down on the river.

"I sure hope he'll see me—if he's not too busy. Hell! I know he'll see me. I have money now and lawyers will always see people with money. I think most lawyers could smell money in a perfume factory. Maybe I should have called, but what the heck. It's right on the way."

Merle walked into the lobby of the large building and stood looking at the directory beside the elevator. "There it is. Paul J. Morgan, Attorney-at-Law, Room 310."

Merle stepped into a large office and was greeted immediately by the receptionist. She was an older lady with a kind, friendly looking face. "May I help you, sir?" "I hope so," Merle replied. "I would like a few minutes with Mr. Morgan if possible." Looking down at the appointment book lying open on her desk, she asked, "Your name, sir?"

"Merle Anderson from Porterville," he replied.

"Merle Anderson. Anderson. Are you any relation to Simon?" she asked.

"Yes, ma'am, I am. I'm Simon's father."

"Well, I'll be! I've never met Simon but I speak with him on the phone quite often. It'll be just a minute," she said. "Mr. Morgan is busy right at this moment, but I'll slip him a note. Please have a seat." She left the room and came back with a tray with coffee, cream and sugar, and a cookie. "He'll be just a few more minutes," she said. "I'm sure he wants to see you." The phone rang. She rushed back to her desk to answer the call.

The door to Paul's office opened. Three men came out talking and laughing as they walked down the hall. "Probably some of Paul's associates," Merle thought as they disappeared into separate rooms along the hallway. Then Paul walked hastily across the room, hand outstretched. "Merle! How in the heck have you been? Haven't seen you since Em's funeral. She was like a mother to me, that woman was. Come on in. Let's visit."

Placing his hand on Merle's shoulder, Paul started to escort Merle into the office with the open door. Paul was a large man with sandy hair, blue eyes, and a big smile. That's what Merle remembered most about Paul—he always seemed to have a smile.

They entered a big office with a huge desk. There were six over-stuffed chairs around a small conference table. A picture of Paul and Simon in Merle's old boat had been enlarged and hung behind the large desk. Sitting down in one of the chairs around the table, Paul motioned Merle to do the same. As Merle settled in his chair, Paul asked, "Are you in trouble, Merle? If so, how can I help?"

Merle shook his head. "No trouble, Paul. Just want you to handle my affairs for me." Then he took the lottery ticket from his shirt pocket and handed it to Paul. "I got the winning number, Paul. Ten million dollars worth."

Paul looked at the winning ticket, whistled softly and said, "Well, I'll be damned. I guess you don't have a usual problem. The only problem I see you have is how to spend it. Do Simon and Peter know of this?"

"No! And I don't want them to know. Fact is, I don't want anyone to know except you and me. That's why I came to you," Merle replied. "I want you to handle all my transactions for me, but first, how do I pick up my money and remain anonymous?"

Paul put his finger to his temple, looked down and thought for a few moments. "I believe you can remain anonymous if you choose to do so, if we can get you in there without a bunch of reporters swarming around. I believe," Paul said, "the best time would be just before lunch. Maybe some of them will disappear by then."

Paul walked around his desk and pushed the button on his intercom. "Shirley! Cancel all my appointments for the rest of the day. Merle and I have things to do."

Paul and Merle sat in silence as they cruised up the freeway. Paul gauged his speed so they would arrive at about the right time. He had also placed a blanket from the trunk on the rear seat for Gus, not wanting to get dog hair on the seat of his new Lincoln Town car.

Paul broke the silence. "Merle, how come you don't want Simon and Peter to know of your good luck?"

"Oh, I don't know," Merle replied. "I guess money has never made anyone very happy. Especially if it's free. Money means a lot more if you earn it. Simon and Peter both have good jobs and they seem to be happy. Neither seems to need any help from me." He went on, "I want you to set up a trust account for the total amount of the lottery money. I want twenty five thousand each year put in an account for each of the boys, ten thousand a year dispensed to me, and with the rest we'll set up a program for a needy town, with needy people. Porterville is the town I have in mind. But Paul, make sure you get your fee up front. I don't want to over-obligate my account. How does that sound to you?"

"Will that be enough for all your needs?" Paul asked.

"I'm sure it will be, Paul," Merle said. "I'm getting up in years and my needs are small. The most important thing for me now is my family and friends."

"I'll have the whole thing set up by Wednesday. Whatever you want after that, just give me a call. I'll keep you up-to-date each month so you'll know exactly where you stand, but what happens if you should die?"

Merle replied, "I want everything to stay the same for the duration of the money. So if I make a long term commitment, nothing can change it. Okay?"

"Merle, I can handle that part now that I know exactly what you want."

There was silence in the car again as Paul pulled into the parking lot of the lottery building. "Here we are," Paul said. "Let's see if we can get this worked out."

There were a few people milling around in the lobby as they approached the reception desk. The receptionist looked up and asked, "May I help you, gentlemen?"

Paul spoke softly. "I am Paul Morgan an attorney. My client has the winning ticket for your lottery. He would like very much to remain anonymous. Please relay that to the person in charge."

She dialed a few numbers on the phone, waited a long moment, then said, "There is an attorney here with his client. They would like to speak to you in private." She waited a few moments for a reply then hung up the phone. "This way, gentlemen."

They were back on the freeway, heading for home. In Merle's hand was a check for four hundred sixty-eight thousand dollars. Merle looked at it again and again and said, "I see it. I believe it, but I still don't feel it. By the way, Paul, could you advance me a couple of hundred dollars until you can get this set up?"

Paul laughed and said, "When we get back you can have the whole office if you want. Yes sir, Merle, you shouldn't have too many worries from now on."

Merle laid back in the seat, closed his eyes and thought to himself, "This has been quite an experience. Yes, quite an experience."

Chapter 4
Putting the Plan to Work

It had been two weeks since Merle had made his trip to the lottery office. Two weeks of having coffee with the guys. After a trip to the clothing store for some new pants, shirts, and shoes and paying the guys back—which none of them wanted to take—Merle went through his checkbook. "What do you know?" he said aloud. "Still more money in here than I've ever had at one time in my whole life. Sure is a good feeling not to be poor anymore."

It was early Saturday morning and just starting to get light out when Merle parked on the street alongside the village cafe. The old pickup had the boat behind. He was going to meet Bob and Walt for breakfast, then they were heading down to Smith River for a day of salmon fishing. This was also the day he would start picking their brains for ideas of what to do for the town and people he needed to help.

Merle was siting at the familiar table by the window about half finished with his first cup of coffee when Walt arrived. "Morning, Walt," Merle said.

"Hi, old man." Walt replied. "Did you bring the net?"

"Yep. I got her this time." Merle said. "After last time I don't think I'll ever forget the net again. That was quite an experience trying to land a thirty-five pound fish with a two dollar gaff hook."

Walt chuckled, "I think if I'd lost that fish, I'd have thrown you and your gaff overboard just for the heck of it." Bob came walking across the room to the table. Walt said, "Look at that, Merle! It's going to take a whole pot of coffee to get him ready for the fishing trip."

Bob replied sleepily, "The wife and I went over to Wayne and Betty's and played cards till after midnight. By the way, Wayne and Bill are going to meet us here and follow us down. Wayne got another motor for his boat and wants to try it out."

It was a beautiful morning as Merle turned the boat up river from the launch ramp. They dropped their lures over the side, let out their lines, set their drags and settled back for a day of fishing on the big river.

The morning was pretty uneventful. Walt had a hit on his line. Bob had one fish on for a few moments, then lost it. Merle just didn't have that fish getting feeling. He had some questions he wanted to ask the guys and do it without giving away any of his plans.

It was around eleven in the morning when Wayne

said, "Bill, let's pull in our lines and run back down and have lunch."

"Suits me," Bill replied. "I've been needing to go to the restroom for quite a while now."

Wayne spun the boat around and headed it back down the river at a pretty good clip. "There's Merle and the guys," Bill said. "Let's see if they want to follow us down and we'll all eat together.

"Remember," Wayne replied, "Walt's in that boat. He has probably eaten everything in there except the bait."

"You could be right," Bill said, "but remember he always brings enough food to feed an army."

As Wayne approached Merle's boat, he slowed his boat down. "Hey, you guys!" he said. "We're going down to the little park and have lunch. You coming?"

"Might as well," Merle said, "not doing any good fishing and I'm having a mild bladder attack."

Sitting around the picnic table under the big maple tree, the five men ate their lunches as they reminisced about past fishing trips, the fish they lost, the ones they caught, the funny things that had happened, and the jokes they'd pulled on each other. Finally Merle changed the subject. "I need some advice. Simon called the other night," he lied. "He works for the federal government you know. He wanted to know how Porterville was doing. Was it improving or was it the same little drab town that he remembered?"

Walt spoke up, "Tell him it's the same little dump.

I don't believe they have changed a light bulb since he's left."

"I know," Merle said, "that's my opinion too. Simon says when he retires he would like to retire here if they could just do something to make it more livable."

Bill spoke, "That would be nice, but most of the people here are so poor that they pool their money just to rent a movie."

Then Bob replied, "What you say is true, Bill, but does it have to be that way? Are all the people like us? We discuss it, we agree on the problems, and then we go home and close the door."

"I don't know about you guys," Wayne said, "but Porterville's going to have to wait, cause I'm going fishing."

The next morning after the coffee break with the guys, Merle drove the old truck down Main Street. There was the park, a large unkept area. "It used to be so beautiful." Merle remembered. "Ha! It sure needs some shrubs and flowers and the grass is going to need a lot of care to get it back in shape. And that old bandstand over there is going to take a lot of repair and paint to make it pretty again. There are three other parks in town. I suppose they are all in this condition."

Main Street looked drab and lifeless as Merle continued slowly through the main part of town. Many store buildings were empty and the ones that were still in business looked as if they had had little or no maintenance for several years. Merle stopped his truck across the street from the big black hole where three buildings had burnt several years ago. "That would take some money," Merle said to himself, "but that could be made into a pretty little plaza. The guys are right, this town sure does need help. I'll give Paul a call in the morning and see if we can start getting some of these things taken care of."

Paul Morgan sat across the desk from Bill Moore, mayor of Porterville. "Mr. Mayor," Paul said, "Please!

Bill Moore replied, "Please, just call me Bill. This town is not big enough or the job important enough for me to be called Mr. Mayor."

"All right, Bill. I'll come right to the point and try not to waste much of your time. I'm Paul Morgan, an attorney from Spring City. I've been sent here by a client who's name I shall not reveal, not now and probably never, although never is a long time. My client has sent me here because he has ideas and money he would like to invest in your community."

"Is the city going to be obligated in any way?" Bill asked.

"No!" Paul replied. "Let me lay the whole program out to you then you can be the judge of that. First, you have four parks in this community. All of them are in need of a lot of attention and repair. We propose a gift of fifty thousand dollars a year for the next twenty years just to be used for the maintenance and beautification of your parks—but there is a catch. Twenty-five thousand will be for labor. We want these people to be older, retired people. The ones that really need to supplement their Social Security or other pensions to have a half-way decent quality of life. There will be no time clocks or any set time they need to work. Just as little or as much as it takes to keep the park that they're responsible for beautiful and in good repair.

"Twenty-five thousand each year will be placed in a parks account for the city. This will be used strictly for the things these people need such as plants, flowers, equipment or anything else. You, or whoever is the mayor, will be in charge of this account and will determine whether one or all of their requests are justified."

"You going to pay the labor?" Bill asked.

"Yes!" Paul replied, "but it will be your decision on who we hire. Fair enough?"

"Sounds great to me," Bill said.

"The second thing we have in mind is a paint fund. We will place ten thousand dollars in a paint fund for the city. Again, this fund will be administered by the city. It will be for any merchant in town that wants to paint and clean up his building. Just paint. No labor. After the first year, this fund will be available to all of the community—houses, fences and so on. Is this a doable thing?"

"I'm sure we can control it very efficiently," Bill said.

"The third thing, Bill, we would like to plant five trees on each block in the downtown hub area. Also, place hanging baskets on all light posts and concrete flower boxes in front of each storefront. They will be made to fit each individual store. We will pay the total cost of this program. Your total responsibility will be to have someone keep them watered in the summer months."

"Can we use some of your park people to do this?" Bill asked.

"No! Of all the things we propose, this is the one thing the city will be responsible for."

"I'm sure the council will have no problem with that," Bill said.

"There's one last thing I'd like to discuss," Paul said. "We have purchased the half block of burnt out property on Main Street. We would like to develop it into a downtown plaza. Here are our architect's drawings and plans for the property." Paul opened his briefcase and handed the plans to Bill.

Bill looked at the plans and whistled softly. "When you people do things, you don't do it just half way. If this is an indication of the other projects, I'm for it one hundred percent."

Paul continued. "The property and improvements will be deeded to the city and will be presented to you at the dedication ceremony upon completion. How's that sound?"

"This is the most wonderful thing that has ever happened or probably will ever happen, but may I ask why? Why is someone doing so much for us?"

"My client loves this town and its people," Paul said. "He doesn't believe it will ever attract more industry or people in its present condition. He says it's going to be a retirement and bedroom community and wants it to be the best in the state."

Paul stood up and extended his hand, which a smiling Bill took heartily. "Tell your client, whoever he may be, that the mayor, the council and the community thank him greatly."

Bill walked Paul to the front entrance. They shook hands again and Bill watched Paul walk across the parking lot. "Unbelievable," Bill said softly, "just unbelievable. And he didn't want to waste my time. . . ."

Chapter 5
A Return Visit

Merle came into the coffee shop a little early this morning, wanting a little time of his own to think of other things he might do with the little bit of uncommitted money he had left. Several days had passed since Paul and Bill Moore had had their meeting. Deep in thought, Merle sat there sipping his coffee. Two men came in and sat at the table behind him. They spoke in low tones of general topics which raised no curiosity from Merle, so he continued in his own thoughts.

He first realized who the men were when the guys started arriving. Walt was the first to speak to that table. "Hi, Mayor. How's things downtown?"

"Pretty good, Walt." Bill Moore said. "A little bit busier since the weathers getting better."

Bob broke in, "Bill! What's this rumor that some rich guy is investing in our town? Is it true or just another of those 'make us feel better rumors'?"

Bill Moore was a small man, in stature—well liked and honest. When he made a statement you could pretty well take it to the bank. Bill replied, "I'll tell

you, Bob. This is one of the best breaks this town has ever had. Yes, it's true and I think there are more good things to come. I'd like to say more, but I'm going to wait until the whole program is presented to the city council. But I'll guarantee you that everything will be known in a few days."

Wayne and Bill came in, followed by Cliff and Jerry. The conversation went from speculation to what if and how come. Merle sat there and listened to the excited talk. "Sure makes a man feel good," he thought.

Merle pulled the old truck into the lane, retrieved his paper, then drove up and stopped at his usual spot by the woodshed. "You know, Gus, this could be the start of something very big in our community."

Merle sat at the kitchen table with the paper spread out before him reading only the articles in which he was interested. This is kinda 'Old Hat,' he thought, after reading a paper in the future. Most of what's in this thing was on television last night. "You know, Gus, this is Thursday. What say, we get up early tomorrow morning and go back up there. Maybe, just maybe, there will be another of these papers of the future."

Merle was up early. After eating bacon and eggs, toast and hot coffee, he picked up his rifle and flashlight and started up the trail. Gus was running ahead looking, sniffing, and lifting his leg ever so often. Again the sand on the cave floor looked undisturbed except where Merle had build his fire. Merle was looking forward to the lovely valley again. Something about it that made you relax and forget all the problems that continue to dominate your memory.

The tunnel was darker this time and Merle was glad that he'd brought the flashlight. The light at the entrance wasn't nearly as bright this time. "Still early," he said, pulling out his pocket watch. "Sure enough, just seven o'clock." Stepping out into the light, Merle saw the sun as it was breaking over the far mountains. The lowest part of the valley was still in darkness.

As he walked down the trail, Merle was fascinated. The sun reflecting off the dew-covered rocks and leaves made it look as if everything was covered with tiny diamonds. Walking on down the trail, he could now see the pool and waterfall. He was almost afraid to look at the bench—afraid there would be no paper. As he slowly turned in that direction, disappointment swept over him. Sure enough, the stone bench was empty.

Merle walked up the few steps to the bench and using his coat sleeve, wiped a spot dry for him and Gus to sit. "It's quite a climb up here," he said. "I think we'll just sit a spell before we start back." Gus had taken his usual position—lying down close to Merle with his head resting on Merle's leg. There Gus was lying in the morning sun, eyes closed, completely relaxed. He looked like he could stay there forever.

Gently rubbing Gus's ears, Merle watched the stub of his tail move back and forth. He knew Gus was willing to stay as long as he did.

Merle sat there for quite some time watching the bees going from sleepy slow motion to full speed. Every bird in the valley seemed to be tuning up their voices for the day's wilderness concert.

"Well, Gus! We'd better be getting back if we're going to meet the guys at nine for coffee." Again, putting his hands down for a boost up, Merle's left hand felt the familiar feel of a newspaper. "What the! This wasn't there when I sat down." Sitting back, he unfolded the paper. "Another Sunday paper. Maybe we can get more help for our friends."

Searching the paper looking for the lottery news,

Merle found the article at the bottom of the inside page. His heart sank. "Not this time, Gus. There are no winners. We might know the future, but can we change it?" He started to fold the paper when something else caught his eye. In bold print he read: "Three winning tickets in the twenty-one million dollar California Lottery. Each ticket worth seven million dollars." "Gus, ya know we could go get that money, but would it be dishonest?"

Returning on the trail back to the house, Merle was walking slower now, deep in thought about what was right and wrong and what he was going to do. Back at the house, he stopped at the woodshed, reached up and removed his pipe and tobacco from the shelf. He then sat down on the chopping block, lit the old pipe, puffed a few times and watched the smoke rise slowly and dissipate in the rafters above. Suddenly Merle stood up. He knew what he was going to do. Time would be close, but he'd have time if everything worked out.

Those three people could be three of his friends. "I can't see where that would be wrong, as long as I don't benefit," he thought. He'd call Paul now and get things moving. After relaying his ideas and wishes to Paul and giving him the names, Merle felt really good inside. "My only doubt," he thought, "is how Walt, Bob, and Bill would handle their prosperity."

Merle spread out the paper on the kitchen table. The headlines which he had paid no attention to before made him suddenly alert. The headlines read: "Earthquake hits small California town. Six people killed and millions in property damage."

Eddieville was a small town in central California. The article went on to say, "Mystery phone call saves hundreds of lives. Radio Station KNTC received a phone call from an unknown person stating that a large earthquake would strike the city at approximately 8:30 P.M."

"Well, I'll be," Merle thought. "That caller must be me, 'cause I'm going to give them a call right now," Merle told Gus as he was picking up the phone, dialing 'O.' "Yes, operator. I'd like the number of Radio Station KNTC in Eddieville, California, please."

In Eddieville, Bill Flynn walked into his office, which looked as untidy as he did. It was not a large room and there was clutter everywhere, which seemed to make the room even smaller. The desk was piled high with ledger books, opened letters and empty envelopes. There was barely just enough room left for a writing space. The telephone was half-buried under old newspapers and clippings. Yes, the room matched the man almost perfectly.

Bill was of medium height and looked as round as he was tall. He must have weighed close to two hundred eighty pounds. Unkempt hair, bushy eyebrows over a ruddy complexion with heavy jowls sagging on his round face gave him an appearance of always frowning. He slipped out of his light jacket and laid it over a stack of boxes at the end of his desk.

Then he sat down carefully in his undersized desk chair. Leaning back and swinging his chair a quarter turn, Bill looked out the big window into the studio control center.

A young man sat at the console playing records, marking pages in his log. Finally after a couple of attempts, he completed a short summary of the local news. "Sure would be nice," Bill thought, "if the schools could at least teach these kids to read."

Jamie White was a young nineteen year old disc jockey—just a year out of high school. When Bill found him, he was bussing tables down at the Cullender Cafe. He wasn't much of a worker, but he liked to talk. He would talk to anyone who would listen. Just what Bill needed—a talker.

Bill was tired. It had been a long thirty-five years in the broadcast business. He had started this little radio station in '63. He figured it would grow with the town. The town never grew much; therefore, neither did his little radio station. Just a little daylight hour station, in a little daylight kinda town.

Bill slid his chair closer to the desk, opened his briefcase and started going through the advertising he had sold the day before. "Well," he thought, "maybe these will at least pay the electric bill." Just then the phone rang. "Hello, KNTC Radio. Bill speaking." He listened for a few seconds, then replied, "You don't say. How do you know this? Who is this anyway?" Bill held the phone to his ear for a few more seconds then slowly hung up the receiver.

Some crack pot, he thought. Said we're going to have an earthquake at 8:30 Saturday night. This was troublesome to Bill. The voice sounded both positive and sincere. Thinking back, Bill remembered that Eddieville had had some mild shakers in the last three months. Bill shrugged his shoulders. Not much I can do about it even if it does happen. But the thought of a major quake left him with both worry and concern for the people of this community.

Bill sat there for a few moments pondering what he had just heard. Looking out over the control room, Bill had a sudden thought hit him. "Hell," he said aloud, "Jamie will be at the high school doing play-by-play of the basketball game. He will be in that little box up next to the rafters. Fact is, that gym will be crammed packed full being the last game of the season and all."

Bill picked up some papers from the desk, pretending to be looking at each one, but his mind just wasn't on his work. So he reached over and picked up the phone, dialed some numbers, then waited for an answer. "Hello, Don," he said, "I have something I need to talk over with you. Could you meet me down at the Cullender for coffee? . . . Okay! About fifteen minutes. Okay, I'll be there." Then Bill hung up the phone, picked up his jacket and left the office.

Leaning over Jamie's shoulder, Bill said, "I'm going to be gone for thirty or forty minutes. You might have to wait a few minutes for your break."

"OK, Bill," Jamie said. "I can handle it. Is there anything wrong?"

"No!" Bill said. "Nothing's wrong."

Bill pulled his car along the curb in front of the Cullender Cafe, walked inside and looked around. "Not here yet," he thought. Walking to a booth back against the far wall. Bill just sat down when Don James arrived.

"Hi, Bill."

"Hi, Don!" Bill replied. Don took his seat across from Bill. The restaurant was almost empty. No one was in listening distance. Don James was the High school principal and also the athletic director. Don and Bill had been friends for years—not good friends, just friends.

"What's up?" Don asked.

"Well, I don't know and I really don't know how to say this without feeling stupid. Anyway here goes." Bill proceeded to tell Don of the phone call and how concerned he was about it.

"It does seem a little scary," Don replied. "What do you think we should do?"

Bill took a sip of coffee then replied, "I would look at this as nothing but a prank call, except I heard his voice. He sounded so confident and direct that the minute I heard I believed it. I don't know why, I just did."

"If you feel so positive about it," Don said, "why don't you go ahead and announce it on the radio?"

"Don, could you see the consequences if I'm

wrong? How many people do you think would show up to your ball game tomorrow night? And how big a fool would I be Sunday morning?"

"I see what you mean," Don replied. "If it did happen it would be during the half-time of the ball game. That place would be packed with people."

"Don, do you suppose we could have a 'bomb scare' just as soon as the first half ends? We could clear the gym of both people and players. We'll get them away from the building. Have them sit in their cars or away from the high walls of the gym. Then if nothing happens, we can call them all back in and no one will be the wiser."

"By golly, Bill. I think that's the smartest thing we could do. We'll still have our game and if done right, no one would be hurt. I'll take care of it on my end. You and Jamie work out a convincing announcement for half time."

Chapter 6

Saturday morning Merle arrived at the coffee shop earlier than usual. He wanted to see if his plan was going to work. Sure enough there were Walt, Bob, and Bill in deep conversation. "Hi, guys," Merle said. "Look at you guys. This is not Sunday and all three of you look as if you're going to church."

Walt spoke first, "Sit down here and tell us what you think." Pulling a letter from his coat pocket and laying it in front of Merle, Walt asked, "What do you make of this?"

Merle pulled the contents from the envelope: a round trip airplane ticket to Sacramento, California, five one hundred dollar bills and a one dollar bill. All of this was wrapped neatly inside a typed letter. Merle went on to read the contents of the typed message.

Dear Friend,
You have lived a life of hard work and honesty. You deserve to be comfortable and happy in your senior years. The numbers below are the winning numbers in the California Lottery: 11-12-16-19-22-31.

Reservations have been made for your
flight and room.
You will be staying at the Capital Motel.
That's directly across from the lottery office.
Buy your ticket first, then enjoy yourself.
Good luck!
Signed, a friend.

P.S. The one thing I do ask is that you
share your good fortune with others in your
community as I have done.

Bill spoke up, "What do you make of it, Merle?"

"Well," Merle replied, "it seems to me the guy
that wrote this letter is either nuts or knows
something we don't."

Bill looked up from his coffee, "All three of us got
this letter. It don't make sense that three of us would
get the same letter."

"Maybe not," Merle said. "Lots of times there's
more than one winner, especially if it's a large
jackpot. I know if it were me, I'd be heading for the
airport as fast as my old truck would get me there."

Bob pushed back his chair and said, "I wonder
if this has any connection with the person that is doing so much for our community?"

"I don't know if it does or not," Merle replied, "but
if any of you guys don't want to go, just give the letter to me. I'll sure the hell go."

"Oh, no you don't! We're on our way. What've we
got to lose?"

"Good luck," Merle said. "Remember me when

you're rich. But beings how you're not rich yet, I'll get the coffee. Have a fun trip."

Walt was looking out the window of the large plane. Deep in his own thoughts thinking, "What if this does happen like the letter said?" All those things he's always wanted to do. The places he's read about or seen on television that he never had the time or money to go see. The mill had provided the needs for his family, but very few of their wants.

He was suddenly removed from his thoughts when Bob said, "We should start down any time now. They said the flight to 'Frisco was only fifty-five minutes." He had no sooner finished his comments when the nose of the plane seemed to roll a little downward. The seat belt light came on and a voice on the intercom. "We will be arriving at San Francisco in about five minutes. Please remain in your seats until the plane has stopped at the boarding area. Thank you for flying United."

Bill had not spoken much on the whole flight. He was a little scared but he wasn't about to let the others know it. "We have an hour layover in 'Frisco," Bob said. "I think I'll see if I can find a lottery machine in the terminal."

"Hey, that's a great idea!" Walt replied. "That way we'll be sure we have them." The plane turned from the taxi area to the large loading tunnel and stopped. "We have an hour," Walt said. "We should be able to find a ticket machine and still have time for a quick coffee break."

The stewardess was coming down the aisle reminding the people getting off to check and make sure they had all their personal belongings. "Excuse me, Miss," Bob said, "do they have lottery machines in the terminal building?"

"Yes, sir! They have a row of them down by the Sky Chief Restaurant. Did you fly here just to play the lottery?"

"No," Bob replied, "just passing through. I heard it's a pretty fair amount."

"Yes!" she said. "I believe it's somewhere around twenty-one million dollars."

"Thank you," Bob replied. "It's been a very good flight."

"Did you hear that, fellows?" Walt said. "Twenty-one million! That's seven million apiece. I didn't have any idea we were talking about that kinda money."

Bill replied, "Twenty million or one million, that's more than I earned in my whole lifetime!" Bob and Walt shook their heads in unison.

"You got that right," Bob said. "You sure got that right!"

Sitting in the motel coffee shop eating their evening meal, the three men looked around. The waitress was a tall, slender, pretty girl, with the bluest eyes that Bob had ever seen. "Miss!" Bob spoke. "Would you happen to know what time they have the lottery drawing?"

"Yes!" she replied. "They show the drawing on channel three at eight o'clock. It doesn't last very long. If you bat your eyes, you'll miss it."

"Thank you, ma'am." Bob replied. "You are a lovely young lady and the food was great."

The three men sat in silence, each with his own thoughts, not knowing how they would accept their success or possibly their failure. Walt spoke first, "Ya know, fellows. This letter is signed a friend. I wonder who it could be?"

Bob replied, "We all have lots of friends, but all of them that I know are just a poor as I am."

"I know," Walt said, "that's the way it is with me too."

Bill spoke up, "The letter also mentioned that we should share our wealth with others. That was pretty explicit."

"If I get any money out of this, I'll do whatever the letter says. Until we do, I don't have much to comment on," was Walt's response.

"We'd better get to our rooms," Bob said. "You get the tip, Walt. Bill and I will pay for the meals."

Sunday morning the three men ate their breakfast in total silence. None of them had slept well. Each was more or less in his own world of disbelief. Walt broke the silence. "We did it fellows. We've won. Now all we've got left to do is keep our part of the bargain."

The little town of Porterville was buzzing with excitement. Three of their own had gone to California.

The same three had come home millionaires. How could it be? How could it happen? How'd they know? It couldn't be just luck, could it? All that the people of Porterville knew for sure was that Old Walt, Old Bob, and Old Bill had gone to California and came home Mr. Turner, Mr. Jones and Mr. Williams.

Chapter 7

Early summer is beautiful in Green Valley. The surrounding hills are covered with different shades of green and the meadows and pastures are painted with wild flowers. This was a sharp contrast to the pot-holed cement, black top and unpainted buildings of Porterville. Compared to Spring City, Porterville was the mud hole of the county. The people of Spring City referred to Porterville as the place that time forgot.

And by rights, they were correct, with one exception. The people of Porterville never forgot to send in their tax money. The forgotten part of it was that they never received much of it back. That's the way it is when the county commissioners forget you every day of the year, except for Election Day.

In a big sunlit room, around a large conference table, five county commissioners sat facing each other. They were discussing the upcoming elections in the fall. Three of the five were running again to save their jobs. Archie, the speaker of the commission, handed a folded up newspaper across to Jack Dunn and said, "What the heck is happening in Porterville?"

"I don't know, Arch. What are you referring to?"

"Read that article that I circled," Archie said.

Jack slid the paper in front of him and started to read.

"Porterville in full swing of their beautification program. The people in Porterville are determined to have the prettiest city in the state."

"Well, I'll be," Jack said. "If they're going to live up to that statement, it'll take lots of work and lots of money."

"Have any of the rest of you read the article?" asked Archie Taylor. As the three other commissioners shook their heads no in unison, Archie added, "Pass it around, Jack, and let them look it over."

After the three had finished the article, Archie asked, "Jack do you have any idea where they're getting the money for this project?"

Jack shook his head and replied, "No, Arch! I haven't the slightest idea. I haven't been down there since last fall."

"Well," Archie said, "that's your district. I believe if it were me, I'd get my buns down there. You're coming up for re-election this fall and without Porterville you can't win."

"I'll run down there tomorrow and nose around. If there's anything serious happening Bill Moore will let me know."

"I wouldn't be too sure of that," Archie said. "I understand that the people down there would like him to run for your seat. If that happens you could be in big trouble. If they're doing all of these things you'd better find a way to use it to your advantage."

"I'll get down there tomorrow and see if I can get in on some of the action," Jack replied.

For the last three weeks, Merle had left home early each morning and driven down Main Street. Each day everything looked a little neater and prettier than the day before. Everyone was doing their job with thought and purpose. There seemed to be pride in everything they'd done. Merle was pleased with the way the town was responding to the beginning of new life that he and Paul had started.

"Look there, Gus. Would you believe six months ago that Main Street would look like this?" The park was just beautiful in the morning sun. The bandstand had been repaired and painted. The grass was manicured so well that it looked like a beautiful green carpet. The walkways were lined with shrubs and flowers in full bloom. In a short time it had gone from something to be ashamed of to a place that was the pride of the community.

Merle stopped his truck across from the not quite completed plaza. There workmen were putting the final touches on the large fountain. This would be the centerpiece of the plaza. Red and white brick fanned out from the fountain giving a sun burst effect. Four five-year-old maple trees had been planted to provide shade for the tables and benches placed near them.

A beautiful Spanish style wrought iron fence sur-

rounded the whole plaza. Over the entrance was a large archway and scrolled on it was the name, "Mystery Plaza 1993." Merle was standing by the entrance rubbing his hand on the smooth finish of the fence, when a well dressed man arrived. He was about the same height and weight as Merle, with black hair and moustache, and dark brown eyes over a small pointed nose. "Hi, there," he said as he approached. "You from around here?"

"Sure am," Merle answered. "Nearly thirty-one years."

The stranger extended his hand to Merle and said, "I'm Jack Dunn, your county commissioner."

Merle shook his hand and thought to himself, "This is the wind bag we've been trying to get rid of." Then he said, "My name's Merle Anderson. Nice to know you, Mr. Dunn."

"You people," Jack said, "have taken on quite a project here in Porterville. Everything is looking just great. I wouldn't have believed the improvement, if I hadn't seen it with my own eyes."

"Yes, it's starting to look pretty nice," Merle responded, "but there's still much to do."

"Are you working on this project?" Jack asked.

"No, I'm not," Merle replied. "I just come down every morning to watch the progress."

"Do you wonder where they're getting the money for all this?" Jack asked.

"We all wonder" Merle answered. "There's rumors that some one or some company in Spring City is putting up the money, but they don't want to be known. Even the mayor doesn't know. They're doing it through some lawyer in Spring City."

"I see," said Jack. "It seems kind of different that someone doesn't take the credit for it."

"I don't know," Merle replied, "some people just don't want notoriety."

"Well, you have a nice day, Merle. It's been good talking to you," Jack said as he walked through the gate toward two of the workmen. Merle stood there listening to the three men talk, making out a word every so often. Then one of the men said. "I think his name is Morgan. Yes, Morgan of Spring City."

As Merle walked back to his old truck, he thought to himself, "I'd better give Paul a call after the coffee break and let him know that he'll probably have a visitor very soon." Pulling the old truck from the curb and continuing on down Main, Merle was becoming very proud of the way the little town was shaping up. On the way back to the coffee shop, Merle drove out of his way to pass through the south neighborhoods. The pride was spreading here too. Houses and fences were being painted. Lawns and flowers took on new priorities with the owners and renters alike. Old cars and appliances disappeared from the streets and driveways. There were almost as many changes in the living areas as there were in town.

"Yes, Gus, our little town is really starting to bloom. My gosh, Gus, I've got so caught up in this that it's almost time for our coffee break."

Merle sat waiting at the table for his friends to arrive. He was real proud of the men he had chosen. They were doing good things with the money. Bill had bought an old building at the far end of Main Street and was remodeling it for a senior center. Bill was a pretty fair carpenter, but he also hired some skilled retired people to work with him. "I'm sure the job they'll do will make that building one of the prettiest in Porterville," Merle thought.

Bill also gave twenty-five percent of his winnings to Wayne and his family. Wayne was also looking for ways to help. Although he hadn't done much yet, he was asking everyone for ideas.

Bob was going a little different direction. He was

doing for the youth. Bob had set up a scholarship program at the high school. He would be giving away ten ten-thousand dollar scholarships a year for the next twenty years, based not so much on test scores but on needs. He remembered how difficult it was to educate his two children. He also gave some of his winnings to Cliff. Cliff was also caught up in the spirit of giving and doing.

Merle was brought out of his thoughts as Walt walked up to the table. "Hi, old man!" Walt said.

"Well, hi, Walter. I didn't see you drive in."

"I got me a new little pickup. The other one was blowing oil so bad that she was about to give up. Besides, I wanted to talk to you before the others arrived. Merle," Walt said, "I don't know how to ask you, but here goes anyway. I would like to share my good fortune with you, as Bob and Bill have done. I would have asked you sooner but I have been afraid to ask. You being so stubborn and all."

"I'm going to be stubborn again, Walt." Merle said. "Now that I get my Social Security, I have more money than I really need. Being a bachelor, I really don't even use all of my check each month. I'd just as soon you shared with someone else who really needs it."

"I kinda figured that would be your answer," Walt replied. "Would you feel offended if I bought you a new pickup to replace that old Chev?"

"I really don't want another pickup, Walt. I bought that truck new before we left Iowa. Em's folks

made the down payment and made the first couple of payments until I started getting my first paychecks. The four of us loaded it down and pulled a little trailer behind with everything we owned."

"Ya, I realize that," Walt said, "but aren't you afraid that it's going to start letting you down?"

"It has a couple of times," Merle said, "nothing serious and it's real easy to work on. I think I know every bolt in it. Besides," Merle explained, "sometimes when I'm driving home, I look across the seat and there's Emma with two little boys between us, all smiling, laughing, singing, and telling stories to pass the miles away. I don't believe that I would find that kinda happiness in any other pickup."

"You always seem to have just the right answer," Walt said, "but I guess if I was in your place, I'd do the same thing. It takes a lot of love to remember so long. Thanks, Merle. At least I gave it my best shot. Would you object if I rented another pickup for a month and took yours down and have it gone through completely? That way, when we go fishing, I can tell my wife that I'll be home for sure," Walt finished with a chuckle.

Merle was getting a little ashamed of saying no to his best friend. "Sure, go ahead," Merle said, "if you really want to."

"I'll have the garage bring one over in the morning during our break and he can take yours, okay?"

"Okay, Walt, but tell him to bring something that Gus can ride in. And Walt, thanks for thinking of me and being my friend."

The other fellows began arriving and the morning's discussions began. Now, not only did they cuss and discuss the weather and fishing but a new topic—things that were being accomplished and ideas to make them better.

The conversation seemed to go on and on, building with excitement and enthusiasm. Finally Walt said, "Sorry, guys. I need to get going. I'm supposed to meet a real estate man over at the River Road Apartments. I'm thinking of buying them and remodeling to make low cost and temporary housing. A place where young people can make a start."

"That'll be great!" Merle said. "It is tough for a

young couple to find a place to live that they can afford." With that the guys started leaving with the "see ya's" and the "so longs." Soon the table was empty.

Outside the coffee shop, Merle walked to the pay phone on the corner, dropped in his coins, dialed and waited for an answer. "Hello, Shirley. This is Merle. Is Paul in? . . . He's not. Well, will you give him a message? . . . Tell him I think he'll have a visitor, a Jack Dunn. He's the commissioner down here. He's nosing around trying to find out everything he can. Tell Paul I don't trust him much. . . . Okay. Thanks, Shirley. Goodbye!"

Chapter 8

Simon sat at his desk stacked high with the morning's reports. After reading each one carefully, signing and making changes as he read, Simon then placed them in different trays on his desk. He laid down his pen, removed his glasses and stood up. Stretching and flexing his cramped fingers, Simon walked slowly to the big window. The small courtyard outside his office was about all the country that Simon had an opportunity to see. D.C. was mostly concrete, blacktop and glass—not a bit like home, nothing like the little valley where he grew up.

Simon was engrossed in his daydreams of home, of Dad and Paul. "Sure would like to see them all again. It's been four years. Things must have changed."

"Mr. Anderson!" came a voice over his desk intercom, startling him back to reality.

"Yes, Nellie," Simon said. "What do you need?"

"Mr. Nelson wants to see you as soon as possible."

"Thanks, Nellie. If he calls again, tell him I'll be down in just a few minutes," Simon replied as he reached for his jacket, straightened his tie and walked from his office.

Putting on his jacket as he walked slowly down the long hall, Simon thought, "What the heck am I doing here? I should be home. Home where there're real places with real people. People who love. People who care. People who can understand a person's feelings."

Simon stopped at the elevator and pushed the bottom button. Waiting for the elevator, he said in a soft voice, "I need a vacation. I need to see Dad. The last time I tried to call, his phone didn't seem to work. I guess I'd better try again when I get home."

Simon stepped into the large room where a pretty red-headed secretary was trying to look busy. "Hi, Joan," he said. "Can I see the old man?"

"Yes! Go on in, Simon. He's expecting you."

John Nelson looked up as Simon entered, motioned with his hand for Simon to sit, as he was looking at a three or four page document. "Simon," John said, "I've got something that I need your help with. I received a letter from the California State Attorney's office. They suspect that they have a lottery fraud. Just speculation mind you. No proof of anything. So they have run into a blank wall and want our assistance. Seems like three men all from the same town in Oregon and all acquainted with each other flew on the same flight to San Francisco and purchased their lottery tickets at the same time—but from different machines. Then they all boarded another flight to Sacramento. All had reservations at the same motel. All three had winning numbers in the lottery. Each picked up his check at the lottery office and all three returned home on the noon flight Sunday."

John continued, "It looks to me like they had advance information. They knew exactly what they wanted to do and how they wanted to do it. It doesn't look like luck or chance. What do you think?"

"Did the authorities talk to these men?" Simon asked.

"Yes!" John replied. "When the men were questioned they all gave the same response. A courier had delivered a letter to each of them Friday evening. In each envelope was a round trip airline ticket, purchased with cash at the airline ticket counter in Spring City. It also contained five hundred dollars in cash. There was also a letter explaining exactly what to do, about the motel reservations and get this—the winning numbers, a day before the drawing. Your thoughts, Simon?"

Simon replied, "My thoughts are the same as yours, John. These people took that trip with one purpose in mind, to bring back the money. It's got the ring of an inside job. Things like that don't happen just by luck, and that's what a lottery is, it's luck."

John stood up and paced back and forth behind his desk. That's where you come in, Simon. You're from Oregon. These men all come from the same town called Porterville. In your file it shows that you are also from that same town. Is that right?"

"Yes, John. I grew up there. My dad still lives in the area, just a couple of miles out of town. By the way, what are these men's names?"

John picked the papers from his desk, flipped to the last page of the letter. "Let's see. Walt Turner, Bob Jones and Bill Williams

"Well! I'll be damned," Simon said. "I know all of those men and all of their families. All three are very close to my dad. There must be a mistake, John. These are the finest, most honest people you'd ever want to know. I don't understand this at all. I'd trust these people with my life. John, let me ask you a question. If you'd received that letter, money, and tickets, and you'd worked hard your whole lifetime and still had very little, what would you have done?"

John thought for a few moments, put a small smile on his face and replied, "I guess, Simon, I'd probably have headed for Sacramento just like they did. So I guess what we need to find out is who wrote that letter and why. And Simon, that is exactly what you're going to do. You and your family will leave day after tomorrow. Make it seem like a visit but give me a full report in two weeks."

"Okay, John," Simon replied, "I'll do my best."

Simon sat at his desk. "What a bizarre thing this is," he thought. "Oh well, it will be somewhat of a vacation. I'll give Paul a call and see if he and Carol can put up with us for a couple of weeks."

It was an early August morning and already getting hot outside when Merle walked into the cool of the cafe. His back and shoulders were stiff and sore. The last couple of days he'd helped put a roof on John Lock's house. This was a returned favor. John had helped him re-roof about ten years ago. At the time he didn't know that John would wait till they were too old to climb the ladder and then when they got up there, couldn't remember what they were up there for. It was hot, hard work, but the two old guys kept after it and had it completed in record time. Too old for that kinda thing he thought. No! Not too old, too lazy maybe. It felt good to work hard again. It made him feel good to think that he was of some use to someone.

The waitress brought Merle a refill of coffee. "Don't look like the boys are coming again this morning," she chatted.

"I haven't been here for a couple of days myself," Merle replied. "Been helping John Lock re-roof his house, so I haven't kept up on what's been happening." Merle pulled out his watch. "They've never been this late before. Wonder what's keeping 'em?"

Nancy replied, "I hear they're taking their coffee breaks over at the Cascade Inn. With all the money floating around, I guess they've outgrown this little place."

"Cascade Inn, hah! Well, I'll be. Why would they do a thing like that? They have terrible coffee over there. Besides that, it's a dollar a cup. Nancy, I'm going on over there and find out what's up. It isn't like them to change years of habit. No! Maybe I'll let it ride a few more days and see what happens. I'm almost sure they'll all be back." Merle seemed to be speaking more to himself than to the waitress.

Merle drove down to Tri-State Garage. Maybe his truck would be finished. As he drove into the service area he noticed a truck just like his. Only this one looked brand new. Larry came out to greet him, "What do you think, Merle? How's she look?"

Merle walked around and around the old pickup. "It's beautiful, Larry," Merle said. "It looks just like it did the day I drove it out brand new!"

"That's the newest old pickup anyone will ever own, Merle. We've rebuilt or replaced all the running gear. Put in a new radiator, new bumpers, seats, mats, glass, wiring, wheels, tires, brakes, drums and paint. I'll tell you one thing, it's a better pickup than the new ones we have on the lot. But the best part for you, Merle, it's all been paid for."

"I know. Thanks a lot, Larry. Come on, Gus! Let's go home."

Driving down Main toward home, Merle, not knowing why, turned right on Ninth Street. He hadn't been out this way for quite a while. After traveling eight or nine blocks, he turned the new, old pickup into a now-deserted old drive-in restaurant. He pulled under the now-sagging canopy, stopped and turned off the engine. Leaning back in the seat in the cool of the canopy shade, Merle closed his eyes and started remembering the way it used to be.

In his mind the little drive-in was bustling with activity. He could see young people with their first cars loaded down with their friends. They were laughing, joking and putting nickels in the music boxes on each post.

There were moms and dads with their back seats loaded down with little children catching a quick meal before a ball game or after the early movie down at the movie house. And on the seat beside him, there was Em, with little Simon and Peter sitting between them. "Yes, miss. We want four burgers, two fries and four small Cokes," Merle said. The sound of his own voice brought him out of his short daydream.

Looking quickly to his right, Merle was half hoping to see his family, but only Gus lay on the seat looking up at Merle with his sad eyes. Reaching over and gently rubbing the back of Gus' head, Merle exclaimed in a shaky voice, "Why does it have to be like that Gus? Why is it when we get old we never think much about the future. We seem to only dwell on the past?"

Tears were swelling in Merle's eyes as the memories of the past were so vivid in his mind. Gus inched over closer to Merle and started licking the back of his hand as if he, too, was feeling the hurt in Merle's heart.

"Thank you, Gus. When everyone else fails me, I know you'll be there." Merle uttered softly while rubbing Gus' ears gently, "Without you, Gus, I'd have nobody. Nobody at all."

Chapter 9

The next morning, Merle walked through the big double doors of the Cascade Inn and stood for a moment to let his eyes adjust to the dimness of the light. "Hey, Merle! Back here." It was Walt standing up so he could be seen. The men sat talking politics and business at two of the large tables. There didn't seem to be the laughing, joking and such that would brighten one's day, like at the Cafe.

Merle walked slowly back to the big tables. Taking a chair between two men that he kind of recognized, but had never met, Merle sat down. Walt spoke first, "Gentlemen, do you all know my friend Merle Anderson?" Several spoke up and said they didn't. Some looked up and never bothered to even comment. With that, Walt started introductions around the tables. Merle shook hands with the ones closest to him and nodded his head for the rest. Coffee and water was placed in front of Merle. With that completed, the conversation drifted back to what it had been before Merle's arrival. There was talk of real estate, C.D. notes, new cars and motor homes.

The coffee break was soon over. Merle finally broke into the last of the conversation. "I'm going down on the river fishing tomorrow. The salmon should be running pretty good. Any of you guys want to come along?"

"I'd like to," Bob said (there was a long silence), "but Bill Arcman has chartered a boat down at the coast for a day of bottom fishing and all of us are pretty well committed to go."

"I know," Walt said, "why don't you come along. Hey, Mr. Arcman is it all right if our friend, Merle, comes along?"

Bill Arcman hesitated for a few moments before he replied, "It would be fine, except I'm afraid we're out of room on the boat. We already have eleven scheduled to go."

"Oh! That's all right fellows. I get seasick," Merle said, "and probably wouldn't enjoy myself anyway."

With that, Bill Arcman stood up. "The coffee's on me. You guys keep getting rich and I'll keep buying the coffee," he said with a chuckle.

Merle, Walt, and Bill were the last to leave. "Nice bunch of guys," Bill said. "All of them are respectable people."

"Nice guys, you bet," Merle said rather sarcastically. "I wonder how nice they'd be if you didn't have money. How was it before? Walt, you and I have been in the bank together. Arcman never once acknowledged that we were even there."

"He just didn't know us then," Walt replied. "Now

that we have money, we're a bigger part of the community."

"How so?" Merle asked. "Are you any smarter now than before the money?"

"No!" Bill said, "but everyone thinks we are."

"We'll see," Merle said. "We'll see. Oh! By the way Walt, they did a beautiful job on my little pickup. Thanks a lot."

"It's the least I could do for a stubborn old friend," Walt replied. They said their goodbyes and walked to their separate vehicles. No longer dusty pickups and older cars. The cars were new, big and shiny.

Merle opened the door on his truck and patted Gus on the head. "You know, Gus, they're still my friends, but they don't seem like best friends anymore."

Paul sat at his desk, and across the desk from him sat Jack Dunn, the commissioner. The formalities were over with and they were ready to get down to business. "What can I do for you Mr. Dunn?" Paul asked.

Jack Dunn hesitated a few moments trying to choose the right words. "I'll come right to the point," he said. "I was in Porterville the earlier part of this week and was amazed at what is being accomplished down there."

"It has been quite a project," Paul said.

"I found out from some of the workmen that you

are promoting and overseeing the whole project."

"Yes," Paul replied. "I am doing it for a client who does not want to be known and I shall keep his wishes until he tells me otherwise."

"I respect that," Jack said. "But what I've come to ask is, is there anything I can do as a commissioner to be part of this project?"

Paul thought for a few moments then responded, "What do you have in mind, Mr. Dunn?"

"I really don't have anything in mind because I don't know what there is left to be done. Not saying I can do anything without the support of the other commissioners."

"What you're trying to tell me then is you can't do anything but still would like to get a little recognition. Is that right?"

"You've pretty well hit it on the head, Mr. Morgan. I guess maybe I'm here to ask for your help. I'm running for re-election this fall and I feel that I'm not too well thought of in Porterville. So I need some recognition to help my image down there."

"You've had eight years to improve your image down there, Mr. Dunn, and what have you done for that area of the county?"

"Not much," Jack replied. "It's almost impossible to get anything past those Spring City commissioners. Seems like if there's extra money they want ninty-five percent of it. It's a tough battle, Mr. Morgan, a tough battle."

Paul was silent for a few moments and said, "Mr.

Dunn, evidently the people of Porterville are not too satisfied with your past performance. We'll give you the opportunity to say the words, but it's up to you to supply the deeds. We're having the dedication of the new plaza next Saturday at 1:00 P.M. You will have the opportunity to speak, probably be the first speaker after the presentation of the deed. How would that be?"

"That's more than fair," Jack replied.

"There will be a very large crowd. You should be able to get your message across. But there's one thing I want you to do."

"What's that?" Jack asked.

"If you make any promises to these people, I expect you to keep those promises."

"Mr. Morgan, thank you very much for letting me participate in your program. I'll do my best not to let you or the people of Porterville down." Jack stood up, shook Paul's hand and said as he left the room, "See you Saturday, and thanks again."

Paul sat back down and finished up a few documents that needed it. He wanted to get out of the office a little early today. He was going down to Porterville and check out the plaza. The dedication is Saturday and he wanted to make sure everything was just right before he turned it over to the city.

Paul picked up his coat and brief case and hurriedly left his office. As he was about halfway through the outer office, he heard the phone ring. Shirley picked it up and answered in her usual professional way. Paul held up his hand and shook his head in a manner making it understood that he did not want to answer. Shirley placed her hand over the mouthpiece just as Paul's hand reached for the outer door. "Paul, it's Simon Anderson. You want me to have him call you later at home?" Paul returned quickly and took the phone from Shirley.

"Simon, glad you called. What's up?"

"Just called to see if you and Carol could put up with me and my family for a couple of weeks."

"Simon, that would be great. Carol and I have missed you and Penny a lot. We sure would like to see those little girls. What time are you arriving?"

"If everything goes right we should be there at 6:15 tomorrow evening, Flight 605."

"Simon, shall I pick up your dad and have him there when you arrive?"

"No! Paul, we'd like to surprise him on his own territory."

"Okay! We'll see you tomorrow then. Have a good flight."

"Thanks, Paul, see you soon."

Paul hung up the phone and turned to Shirley. "How's that for timing? He'll be here for all the excitement that his dad has caused and I won't even be able to tell him. Shirley, see if you can get a hold of Peter. His address and phone are in his file. Use whatever excuse you want, but get him here."

"I'll try, Paul," Shirley said. "I'll really try."

The large plane leveled off as the pilot cut back on the powerful engines. They went from a loud roar to a muffled, soothing hum. Penny was reading a travel brochure, while the girls were giggling and playing a game that they'd bought for the trip. Simon leaned back and closed his eyes. The sound of the engines was almost hypnotic as he slipped off into deep thought.

His thoughts returned to his last years of law school. School was quite hard for Simon. He remembered having to quit his part time job just to concentrate on his studies. Corporate law was tough for him, but that was what he wanted so that's what his dad wanted. His dad said to him often, "You do the studying, I'll do the working. We'll get you through that place somehow." And Paul, just the opposite, was easygoing, first with a joke, always having a laugh or smile. Things came easy for Paul who was serious only when he had to be and studied just enough to get by. Paul was a third generation lawyer, and his father provided well for him while he was in school.

Paul had all of his needs taken care of and most of his wants. Not so for Simon. Dad had worked hard, saved every cent so he and Peter could go to college. Hours meant nothing to his dad. If there was extra work, Dad was first in line. Often he heard his dad tell his friends, "My boys are going to get an education, come hell or high water."

Simon spoke without opening his eyes, "Penny,

do you like what we're doing? Do you like where we live? Sometimes do you get homesick like I do?''

"Yes, Simon, I do!'' she said. "But if you like your job and surroundings, then the girls and I are happy, too. Although the girls are getting to the age now where there could be some concern, not problem wise, mind you. It's just that private school all day and a fourth floor apartment for a home. They are growing in size and knowledge but not socially. You know what I mean?''

"Yes, I do, honey,'' he said. "I've been thinking the same thing for quite a while now. Julie will be thirteen, Jill ten and Jessica. . . . What's she? Seven or eight? Oh, yes. Eight. We just had her birthday. Anyway I don't believe they're getting a chance at a real life, like other children, like we did when we were that age. Those ages could be the happiest years of their lives if given a chance.

"What can we do about it?'' Penny asked.

Simon did not answer. He just sat there deep in his thoughts as the large plane raced through the sky. Finally he said, "We're going home!''

Chapter 10

Paul and Bill Moore were standing inside the plaza gate watching the workmen setting up the bleachers and putting the final touches on the speakers' platform. "Paul, the city of Porterville is very grateful to you and your partner," Bill said, "for this plaza, for the ideas, the workmen and the money. We'll always be grateful. It has already been wonderful for our town and its spirit."

"By the way," Paul said, "I have a couple of favors to ask."

"It's your show," Bill replied. "I'll do anything you'd like me to do."

"No!" Paul replied. "It's our show, Bill. What we do, we'll do together."

Bill Moore thought to himself, damn, I like this guy, then said, "What favor do you need, Paul?"

"First, I have promised Jack Dunn that he could say a few words." Paul watched Bill's face as he spoke. Frown lines formed there as Paul continued. "I knew it! I can tell by your face that you really don't approve."

"Did it show that bad?" Bill asked.

"Anyway, I know he's not too well thought of and

I just have an idea that he is going to try to take some of the credit for this program and if he does, he'll put his foot right in his mouth."

"That I'd like to see," Bill exclaimed. "That I'd like to see."

"The reason I know this," Paul said, "is that the next speaker I've asked to address us is a friend of mine. He's an attorney from Washington, D.C., Simon Anderson. He grew up here in Porterville. His dad is Merle Anderson. I believe you know him."

"Yes," Bill said. "I know him, but not as well as I know his friends. There's a strong bond in that group of men. Their friendship is kinda the envy of the whole community."

"Simon is quite an important person in the State Justice Department," Paul said. "And I know Merle would be real proud to hear him say a few words. Also, I'm filling Simon in on this Dunn fellow. If anyone can put him in his place Simon can, and will."

"That'll be great. I'd even pay to see that," Bill chuckled. "I'd hate you to think I'm prying, but would he be the one that's providing all this for us?"

"No comment, Bill. No comment."

Later that evening Paul and Simon were sitting on the patio watching Carol, Penny and the girls swim and frolic in the large pool. The two men had been visiting, catching up on everything that happened since their last meeting. But now they watched in silence. Each was deep in his own thoughts.

Simon was comparing the quality of life that Paul and Carol had to that of his own family with the fast, unfriendly pace of Washington, D.C. This is the easy-going life he remembered. This is the life he wanted again for Penny, himself and the girls.

Paul, too, was putting his thoughts together, wondering about tomorrow, about Jack Dunn, the plaza, the excitement and how to approach Simon to say a few words. Carol interrupted their thoughts as she approached and said, "Honey, if you'll light the barbecue, the girls and I will get dressed and start fixing the salads."

As Penny walked by, she stopped and took Simon's hand, looked into his eyes and said, "I love it here, honey. I really do."

Simon gently squeezed her hand. "Me too, Penny. I think this is where we belong."

In the meantime, Paul had moved over to the far end of the patio and was lighting the barbecue. On his return, he stopped at the small bar and poured two glasses of cold lemonade to bring back to the table. He set one in front of Simon and sipped on the other as he returned to his chair. Paul put his glass down and looked into Simon's face. "You've been pretty quiet since you've been here Simon. Is there something troubling you?"

"A little bit," Simon replied. "I have something I want you to read. Maybe you can help me with it. I'll be right back." Simon rose and hurriedly walked into the house.

Paul was both worried and confused. What problem could keep Simon from being his old self? He did not have long to wait as Simon returned with a letter in hand and laid it in front of Paul. Paul took the letter and slowly read it page by page. He then looked up at Simon. "This isn't a vacation, is it? You're here to find out about this."

"Yes, I am," Simon replied. "It's probably the hardest job I've ever had. Those men mentioned in that letter are good friends of my dad and also of mine. If this letter is correct, it looks like these old fellows are mixed up in some kinda fraud. This is where I need your help. Maybe between the two of us we can find out who's behind this without hurting these men too much."

Paul looked down at the paper in his hand, not reading it, just stalling for a little time to think. Picking up the cellular phone on the table and dialing the numbers, Paul spoke, "Maybe we can get this straightened out now." Paul held the phone to his ear. It seemed like it rang a long time. He was about to hang up when a "hello" came through the receiver. "Hello, this is Paul."

"Hi, Paul," came the response. "What's up?"

Paul replied, "There's a man here from the federal government. It seems like we're being investigated. I recommend we reveal all we know just to keep us out of trouble."

There was a long silence before Merle replied in a quiet, shaky voice, "I guess it'll be all right. I seem to have lost all my friends anyway, so it really doesn't matter anymore."

"You still have us," Paul answered. "Remember that!"

"I will, Paul. Thanks. I surely will."

"I'll see you tomorrow," Paul said. "And keep your chin up."

"What was that all about?" Simon asked.

"I got a long story to tell," Paul said. "But I don't know all of it. Only one person does."

"Who's that?" Simon asked.

Paul placed his hand on Simon's arm and replied, "Your dad, Simon. Your dad."

"Oh, no!" Simon gasped. "Paul, tell me everything that's happened. Paul, please. I want to know it all."

Paul began telling everything that had happened from the day Merle walked into his office and proceeded detail by detail right up to the phone call that he'd just made.

"So that was my dad you just talked with and the reason he kept it a secret was on account of his friends."

Yes," Paul said. "That's the sad part! When they got money, he lost them anyway."

"You know, Paul, in my whole lifetime I've never known my dad to be dishonest or even to lie, so everything you told me sounds like something he would do." Tears came to Simon's eyes. "I always thought he was quite saintly, but never did it cross my mind that he could be a prophet. That has to be it. Paul, tell me that has to be it!"

"Another thing that I didn't mention," Paul continued. "Did you read about the earthquake in California? Well, that was the same weekend we sent his friends to California. I don't know if it has any connection but the paper said a mysterious phone call saved hundreds of lives. I don't know, Simon, if your dad's a prophet. I hope so, but that part you'll just have to ask him."

Carol came out with a platter of uncooked steaks. As she approached, Paul rose and took them from her and walked to the barbecue, speaking back over his shoulder. "By the way Simon, after dinner I have a business deal to discuss with you."

"That's good, Paul!" Simon replied. "After writing a bizarre report on all of this I'll probably need some kind of business deal."

Paul chuckled, "I'm glad it's you that has to write it."

Merle sat alone at the big table glancing from the clock above the serving window to the parking lot every few minutes. Linda came up and was pouring his refill when he said, "Quarter after nine; guess the guys are still going over to the other place. I just don't like the coffee over there and the waitresses aren't nearly as cute."

Linda smiled, "You old fox! Keep it up and you're just liable to walk out of here with a free cup of coffee." She laughed softly as she moved away.

Merle, staring down at his coffee, thought about what Paul had said on the phone. He felt confident that he'd done nothing illegal, but that was not for him to say. He'd tell his story to the federal guy and let the chips fall where they may. I'm sure they won't put me in jail too long, he thought. All I've tried to do is help. Oh, well, he sighed, it doesn't matter anyway.

Suddenly the shouts "Grampa! Grampa!" caused Merle to look up and see three little girls racing across the restaurant with arms outstretched and happy faces everywhere. Merle rose from his chair and stooped down toward the girls. "Well, I'll be," was all he could say before he was showered with hugs and kisses. Merle stood up after kissing the top of Jessica's head. There, walking across the room, were Penny, Simon and Paul. As the three approached, Merle stretched out both arms. Simon did the same. The two men happily embraced in the middle of the Village Cafe. Simon patted Merle on the back as they embraced, "I love you, Dad."

"I love you too, Son. Welcome home."

The reunion was joyous, with laughter, tears, and stories of Washington, D.C., the flight, the night at Paul and Carol's with the big swimming pool. The girls left out nothing. After a few minutes the excitement and the stories starting slowing down. The girls were starting to get restless, not wanting to sit still. Simon spoke, "Penny, why don't you take the girls and show them around town? Dad, Paul and I have things we need to discuss. And honey, make sure to be at the plaza before one o'clock."

"Okay, dear. Bye, Dad. See you guys later."

"Bye, Grampa. Bye, Grampa. Bye, Grampa," the girls were saying as they were going out the door.

"Merle," Paul said, "you can no longer be the ghost of Porterville. Simon is the government man I told you about last night. The reason he is here is to see if there's any fraud in any of this. Until last evening he had no idea you were involved in any way. All he knew about was Walt, Bill and Bob. Make it easy on him, Merle. It's a tough job when the people involved are his and your friends. It's doubly tough to question his own father."

Merle was looking down at the table as Paul was talking, feeling like a youngster getting scolded for doing something bad. Merle looked up at Paul, then to Simon, then back to Paul. "I told you the reason I didn't want to be known. I didn't want that money to come between me and my friends. If I'd just let things be after the first event everything would be just fine. But, no! I didn't want them to struggle through their old age."

"About the numbers," Merle said, "and how I got them is a long story. Sit back and listen. I'll tell you the whole story, then you can judge me, if I did wrong or not." Merle then proceeded to tell the story of the day he discovered the paper, the valley and the stone bench. Both men sat in total silence as Merle told them every detail of the two trips to the valley, leaving out nothing, including the earthquake call. "Well, there you have it. I know it sounds bizarre, but that's the way it was and I'll swear by it."

Both men sat in silence for a few more moments trying to digest in their minds what they'd just heard. Then Simon said, "That's quite a story, Dad. If you say it happened that way then that's the way it happened. Right, Paul?"

"You bet, Simon. That's the way it happened."

"Dad," Simon spoke, "you mean all your friends deserted you once they came into money?"

"Not really deserted me," Merle replied. "They're just too busy with their own projects. You'll see them all today. They'll be sitting in the front row. They're pillars of the community now."

"Come on, Merle," Paul said. "Lets show Simon around town. Let him see what we've done."

As they got up to leave, Merle reached for his billfold. Linda spoke up, "No, you don't Merle. The drinks are on me. It's good to see you happy again."

"Thanks, Linda," Merle replied. "I'll see you at the dedication?"

"Wouldn't miss it," she said.

Chapter 11

Jack Dunn was standing by the entrance of the plaza, greeting and shaking hands with all as they arrived. "This'll be a piece of cake," he thought. "My only opponent is not even here and if he does show up, his name isn't on the program. Yep, old Larry Price, with all his money, is not going to slow me down on my re-election bid."

So on this day, Jack was going to be the center of attention. He'd give these little people a promise or two. He'd tell them what a little money, ideas and effort could do and if re-elected that this was only the beginning. "Yes, Sir!" he thought, "with this crowd behind me, I could be a shoe-in."

Meanwhile, down at City Hall, Larry Price and Bill Moore were walking out the front entrance. "The news you gave me is just wonderful, Larry," Bill said. "If you don't mind, I think this would be a good time to announce it. Are you sure you don't want to say a few words at the dedication?"

"I'm sure," Larry said. "I've been a worker and a doer my whole life. Never been much of a talker. Thanks anyway, Bill. This is your day—yours and your community's."

"I know," Bill said, "but Jack Dunn is going to blow his horn; however, I think before the day is over, he'll probably wish he hadn't." The two men walked slowly toward the plaza, stopping every so often to look at the flowers, trees and hanging baskets.

Merle picked up Gus from the front seat and placed him in the back of the pickup. "Sorry, old fellow, you'll have to ride back here for a while." Taking an old towel from behind the seat and carefully wiping it down, Merle spoke to Simon and Paul, "Don't want you city dudes getting your britches dirty."

"This old truck looks just like new," Simon said. "Looks like it did when I was growing up."

"Looks pretty nice, don't it? Walt had it all fixed up and painted for me."

"Oh, so you still have one friend left?" Simon asked.

"Yes, they're all still my friends. They're just so busy that they don't have time to be best friends anymore," Merle replied.

"We still have forty minutes, Merle. Let's give Simon a tour of the town," Paul suggested. So Merle drove the new, old truck through the neighborhoods of newly trimmed lawns, painted fences and houses, by the parks and down Main Street by the plaza.

"Well, Simon, what do you think?" asked Merle.

"Compared to the Porterville that I once knew, it's unbelievable. It's beautiful. Dad, did you know it would turn out like this when you first started?"

"No, Son," Merle replied. "I had no idea that the people of the community would or could afford to do the things that they've done. By the way, Paul, I haven't see Carol. Didn't she come down with you?"

"No, Merle, but she'll be here in time for the dedication," Paul replied.

Merle found a place to park a couple of blocks from the plaza. "Never seen this many people in town before," he said.

Simon winked at Paul and said, "I think the old man is happy again."

"How could I not be happy," Merle replied. "All my dreams are coming true."

After getting out, Merle put Gus down on the sidewalk. "You guys go on ahead. I'd better let this old dog walk around a few minutes and do his duty."

"I suppose we'd better," Paul said. "We both should get there a little early and look at the schedule."

Simon placed his hand on Merle's shoulder. "Don't be late, Dad. We need your support."

"I'll be there," Merle said. "I wouldn't miss this for anything."

After letting Gus run for a few minutes, Merle placed him back on the pickup seat. "The afternoon could be long and hot, Gus. It'll be cooler in here." With that, Merle turned and walked slowly down the street.

Jack Dunn was still shaking hands with all who arrived and beginning to wonder if the people would ever quit coming. The extra pounds that he'd gained over the last couple of years were starting to take their toll on his feet and legs.

Glancing down the sidewalk to see how many more people were arriving, he saw two tall, well dressed men approaching. He could tell by the way they walked and carried themselves that these were men of education, of confidence and importance. Suddenly Jack could feel his too-tight pants and jacket. He also could feel his unbuttoned shirt collar and loosened tie. But what he could feel most of all was his confidence slipping. "Who could these guys be?" he thought. As they came closer, Jack finally recognized Paul Morgan. "Who's the other guy?" he wondered to himself.

As Paul and Simon approached, Jack took a few steps toward them and extended his hand. "Mr. Morgan," he said.

"Mr. Dunn," Paul replied. "I'd like you to meet Mr. Simon Anderson. He's with the Justice Department in Washington, D.C."

With his confidence on the decline, Jack gave Simon a limp hand. As Simon shook Jack's hand his piercing blue eyes seemed to look right through Jack. What he saw was a man without too much substance and, at that moment, no confidence at all. What Jack saw was a strong, confident man. A man who would not be fooled a bit by his prepared speech.

"I suppose we'd better get up there," Paul said.

"I see Bill Moore is already on the platform. I want you to meet him, Simon, before we get started."

"Are you going to speak today?" Jack asked, looking at Simon.

"Yes," Paul replied before Simon could. "He's our main speaker, so I'd like for you to hold your speech to ten or fifteen minutes, if you will."

Jack didn't reply. He just turned and walked toward the platform. "I'm the county commissioner," he thought to himself. "I should be the main speaker. Who is that guy? What's he doing here anyway?" Jack climbed the stairs and was about to take a seat next to Bill Moore when he noticed a sign on the seat, 'Reserved for Paul Morgan'. The next seat had Simon Anderson's name on it. Jack looked at every empty seat and found his at the very end of the row. As he took his seat, he spoke to himself, "Seems like I should be closer than the council members. They're not important."

The plaza was completely full when Merle arrived. He found a spot back by the entrance where he could stand. By standing there he could see all and Merle wanted to miss nothing.

He had been standing there for a few minutes when he heard someone next to him speak, "Hello, Dad."

Turning Merle looked into the face of a smiling Peter! The reunion was much the same as it had been with Simon. The men embraced with teary eyes. Neither could find the right words. On the third embrace, Peter broke the silence, "Dad, there's some-one I'd like you to meet."

Merle's eyes followed Peter's glance. Faintly he heard Peter say, "This is Emily Clark, my fiancé." Merle looked into Emily's face. His heart almost stopped. There stood his Em of thirty five years ago—same eyes, same face, same turned-up nose. Merle was so emotional that he reached out and pulled her to him. Hugging her gently he spoke softly, "Welcome home, Em."

Peter broke in and said, "Remember, Dad. I said I'd never marry until I could find a wife like Mom. Well, here she is and we're very much in love."

"You sure did, Son," Merle said. "You sure did."

"Dad," Peter said, "Emily's from Kansas. Her folks are wheat farmers outside of Cunningham, a small town mid-state. She's with a dance troupe that has been performing in 'Frisco. That's where I met her and I haven't let her be since."

"Hang on, Son," Merle said. "Hang on and never let her go. She's beautiful."

Emily flushed a little bit and looked into Merle's face and said, "You're so much like my dad, I know I'll be happy in your family."

"Thank you, Emily," Merle answered, "thank you very much."

Carol, stepping around Peter and Emily, said, "Penny and the girls are saving us some seats. We'd better take them before someone else does." Peter replied, "You girls go ahead. Dad and I'll be there in a minute. Isn't she something, Dad?"

"She sure is," Merle replied. "When are you getting married?"

"The middle of next month," Peter replied. "She's given her notice to the troupe and I'm taking a two week vacation, the second and third weeks of September. We plan to get married here in our little church. But now we'd better go sit."

"No!" Merle replied. "You go ahead. I'm too excited to sit anywhere."

"Okay," Peter said. "Don't sneak out on us. I want to see more of you before we leave."

"Leave?" Merle asked.

"Yes, leave," Peter replied. "We have to catch the six o'clock flight. Emily has a performance at nine tonight, so we'll need to leave shortly after things are over."

"I see," Merle said quietly. "I'll be here."

Merle stood there with pride as Peter walked down the aisle to meet the girls. And there was Simon sitting on the platform. How fortunate he was to be their father. Just then the program began with the high school choir singing the "Battle Hymn of the Republic."

"Mine eyes have seen the glory. . . . "

Chapter 12

Minister Coy Reed had just finished a much too long opening prayer when the choir began another song—"This land is your land, this land is my land. . . ." As the song continued, Simon looked out over the crowded plaza. There in the first row of seats sat some of his dad's friends. He recognized Walt, Bill and their families; Bob, Wayne, and their wives; and Bill Moore's wife and children.

In the second row he saw Penny, Carol, Peter and the girls. Looking on over the crowd, Simon discovered he was recognizing faces but not remembering the names. Suddenly his eyes went back to Peter. The woman setting beside him sure looked familiar. Simon was sure he had seen her somewhere before.

"Do you know who that woman is sitting beside Peter?" he asked.

"That's Peter's fiance," Paul replied. "Shirley told me he was bringing her along."

"His fiancé, huh! Why does she look so familiar?" He started digging back into his memory and thought, "That's it! That girl resembles Mother."

Simon, turning again to Paul, "That girl looks just like my mother, when she was young. Peter did it. He found a girl just like Mom."

Paul looked hard at Emily. "Sure enough. She does look like your mother. I wonder what Merle thought when he saw her?"

Simon's eyes continued looking out over the plaza. There standing back by the exit was his dad. "He never did like crowds," he thought to himself. "He wants to be where he can get out in a hurry." As he continued looking around, Simon's gaze paused on the front row and he thought, "It doesn't seem like Dad's friends even recognize me. Have I changed that much?"

As the music concluded and the applause died down, Bill Moore walked to the podium. He shuffled some papers as he laid them out before him and began to speak. "Citizens of Porterville, visitors, and guests, I'd like to extend a welcome to you from the City Council and myself. Next, I'd like to explain the plaza's name, 'Mystery Plaza'. Knowing who provided this beautiful plaza for us is a mystery to all of us, and until such a time that it is revealed, it will remain a mystery. That's why we named it 'Mystery Plaza.'

"Before I turn this over to the guest speaker, I have a couple of important announcements to make. First I would like to mention that I have just been informed by Mr. Baker of the planning commission that a major developer has taken option on the old Burgerville site and the surrounding properties. They are planning a center of twenty-seven stores. Three of these stores will be major retailers. This will give a major boost to the retail and shopping district of Porterville."

After the applause that filled the plaza died down from that announcement, Bill continued. "The other good news that I'd like to share with you is this. I just came from a meeting with Mr. Price, of Price Lumber Company of Tall Firs. Many of you know that Mr. Price owns thirty acres just east of our city limits. Next month his company is starting construction on a new door and window factory on that site. This will be a ten million dollar project and, when completed, will employ one hundred fifty men and women in our community. How about that? Things are looking up for all of us."

That announcement brought the whole plaza to their feet at once—applauding, shouting, and slapping each other on the backs. After the plaza quieted somewhat, Bill Moore continued, "Mr. Price is in the audience today. He didn't want to speak; he said that this was our day. That this was a day for the people of Porterville. Thanks again, Mr. Price, for choosing our town." Again the crowd broke into a long, enthusiastic standing ovation.

As the applause continued, there was one man not happy, not standing, and not applauding. That was Jack Dunn. The news had shaken him clear to his toes. Not only had he lost his confidence but now

he didn't even have a horn to blow. What was he to say? What was he to do? The speech that he held in his hand was worthless. Words did not come easy for Jack. That is why he had to plan, prepare and rehearse before each speech, and now he was lost. What made it even worse, he was the next speaker.

He was brought back to the moment when Bill Moore said, "And your next speaker is Commissioner Jack Dunn." There was a sprinkling of applause as Jack approached the podium. He had wadded up his speech and left it on his chair, so he was about as unprepared as any politician had ever been.

Jack spoke in a quiet subdued voice. "Mr. Mayor, members of the council, and ladies and gentlemen of Porterville. First, I'd like to compliment your city government and you people of Porterville for a job well done. Your town is just beautiful, and the way you have it planned, it should remain this way for years to come. I can understand why a developer would choose a city such as this. A city full of ideas, enthusiasm, and action. I am sure that Mr. Price also saw those same merits as he chose this community for his new factory. Everything I've seen here today has been positive. I see a town that's growing up to be a city."

Jack became very humble in both manner and voice as he continued. "I came here today on the advice of my political brothers in Spring City. I came here today to convince you of what a good commissioner I have been and, like all politicians, take some of the credit for what is happening here. But I can't. As I shook your hands and looked into your faces, I saw hard-working, honest people. People who had fallen into economic hard times, but still had hope for a better tomorrow. This type of people you can't deceive with untruths. So, I'm giving it to you as straight as I can. For eight years I've been your commissioner. In those eight years I've accomplished very little. As of right now, I don't deserve your vote, but if you do decide to let me stay, I'll give 'em hell up there in Spring City and never let you down again. Remember on this day someone cared enough to give you a second chance. I hope you people will care enough to give me one. Thank you."

The crowd in the plaza applauded loudly as Jack made his way down the aisle to the exit. Bill Moore turned to Paul and said, "Well, I'll be damned!" As Jack approached the exit, Larry Price stepped in front of him and extended his hand. As Jack took his hand Larry said, "Jack! The only thing we ever wanted from our commissioner was someone to look out for our interests. Someone with backbone enough to stand up to those guys in Spring City. I think you found yours today. Today I've decided to quit the commissioner race. I really don't have time for it and today I think we've found a new Jack Dunn to replace the old Jack Dunn. Good luck!"

"Thanks, Mr. Price," Jack said. "Today I found out what it's like to be with real people."

Bill Moore again stood before the podium. "The

speaker that I'd like to introduce is one of the people responsible for everything that you see happening in Porterville. He and his partner have used their ideas and money to start, and complete, this whole project. Please give a big welcome to Paul Morgan." Bill turned and looked at Paul as Paul approached the podium. Bill smiled and gave Paul a wink and said in a low voice that only Paul could hear, "Go to it. And Paul, don't give me any more surprises like the last one!"

Paul shook the mayor's hand and stood before the people for a moment before he spoke in a soft, gentle voice—like he would in a conversation with friends. "Seven months ago a very good friend sat with me in my office telling me of his love for this town and its people—you, his friends. He had the money and the vision of what he wanted to do for this community. Look around you and you can see his dream. He has other ideas and dreams to bring forth. These will come soon enough as money is available. I am but a tool that he has selected to mold this all together. The plaza is completed and is ready to be turned over to your city."

Paul turned and looked at Bill Moore and said, "Bill, come and stand beside me." Bill rose and took his place beside Paul.

Paul spoke again. "Mr. Mayor, I have been commissioned by the person responsible for this plaza to present to the city of Porterville the deed to this property and all improvements that have been made upon it." Paul then took the large envelope and handed it to the mayor.

Bill responded with, "Thank you, Mr. Morgan, from myself and all the people of Porterville." The plaza again erupted in a standing ovation. When the applause started quieting down and people returned to their seats, Bill Moore also returned to his.

Paul turned and again addressed the people in the plaza. "I know the day is getting warm and you are probably getting tired of words, but I would like to say a few words about our next speaker. This man is a very special friend of mine. He is presently with the Justice Department in Washington, D.C. He is a local man who has reached the very heights of his profession, and Merle, I hope you hear this—he is soon to be my law partner with offices in Spring City and Porterville. Give a big welcome to Mr. Simon Anderson!"

The people were again applauding, mostly out of respect and name familiarity. As Simon walked to the podium, he gave a smile and a wave to his family and friends in the front rows. Looking over the people, giving waves of recognition until he spotted Merle and gave him the thumbs up sign. That was the favorite sign of his dad's when Peter or himself did something of which he approved.

Walt turned to Bob, "Well, I'll be damned. That's Simon. I didn't even recognize the kid. I'll bet Merle is awfully proud today."

"I didn't recognize him either," Bob replied. "He

sure has changed since I saw him last. Must have been four or five years ago."

"Yah, at least that," Walt said. "I think the last time he was home was for his mother's funeral."

Back by the fence, Merle stood proudly. Tears moistened the corners of his eyes. "He's coming home," he said to himself. "My family's coming home for good." Just then something touched his hand. As he glanced down, Merle found he was looking into the face of Jessica. Reaching down, he picked her up and gave her a gentle hug.

"Why are you crying, Grampa? Why are you sad?"

"These are not tears because I'm sad, Jess. These are tears of happiness. You're moving home."

"I know, Grampa. Isn't it exciting?"

The applause quieted down and Simon concentrated on his thoughts and began to speak. "Mr. Mayor, people of Porterville, I want to thank you for this chance to speak. I'll try not to speak too long, but the things I have to say really need to be said. You listen and form your own opinion of whether we're right or wrong.

"Several months ago, I wrote my father, wanting to know about Porterville. I wanted to know about Porterville and you people. I told my dad that I'd like to come back, but only if things were changing for the better. I needed a place where Penny and myself could raise our family in a clean, progressive environment. And believe me, after seeing this town and you all again, the decision was not difficult to make. We'll be moving back as soon as possible.

"The second reason that I'm here is to inform you of what has happened here, why it happened and who was involved. Think back with me to eight months ago. The largest jackpot in Oregon's history was won by an unnamed person. This person wanted it that way. He just didn't want it to be known; so therefore, the lottery people complied with his request, so this event just quietly faded into history.

"This person then hired his long time friend, Paul Morgan, and his firm to administer these funds to his wishes. What you see today is the fulfillment of some of those wishes. I know there're many questions you'd like to ask, but let me continue and many of them I'll answer for you.

"Why did he do this? Why not enjoy his money? Why not let people know of his wealth? That way he could take his proper place, with the prominent people of this community. I hope to answer all these questions in the next few minutes."

There was total silence throughout the whole plaza. People were giving their complete attention, not wanting to miss even a word. They were listening for an answer to what had been a mystery to all of them for months.

Simon continued, "This person had a lot to thank this community for. This was where he worked and raised his family. The schools gave his children an education. The doctors healed them when they were sick. The churches lifted their spirits and helped them through the rough times in their lives.

"You see, he felt protected here. This was his town. You were his friends. This was home. After the mills closed, this community fell on hard times. His heart ached for the people and town he loved. He felt sorry for the businesses that had to close. He hurt for the people that had to do without, especially since he was a member of that group. He felt extra sorry for the older people. Many of them were too young to retire and too old to find work. He watched as their savings vanished and the quality of their lives eroded.

"These are the things he felt. These are the things he saw, so when he did come into this money, these were the things and the people he wanted to help to make things better.

"Why did he want to remain unknown? Simple. Past history tells us that nothing comes between friends faster than the wedge of money. Some say this is not true, but the truth is, money changes lifestyles and lifestyles are full of little wedges separating you from your past.

"He had a vision for this town. A place where everyone was friends — the rich and the poor, the young and the old, the working and the unemployed. He wanted to use his money to do something for all of these people and according to the things that Bill Moore spoke of today, these things are starting to happen.

"Through this same vision three of his best friends unknowingly took his advice. All three became overnight millionaires. But now his plans are falling apart. The same fears that kept him anonymous have been realized through these friends. After receiving their wealth, they did not respond in the same way. Yes, they started drifting away from those long years of friendship and all of this was that age-old wedge—the standard of money. You, who know of what I speak, ask yourself if this is not so."

Simon stopped his talk for a moment and took a sip of cool water. There was a murmur running through in the crowd. People were looking at each other, wondering who and why. Walt, Bob and Bill sat stone still looking neither right nor left, just straight ahead. All three were deep in their own thoughts. Each one knew for sure that Simon was speaking about him. All three really believing that Simon was wrong, that they hadn't changed at all.

Simon brought everyone's attention back as he continued, "So, now you have the story. All of you here now, ask yourself this question, 'Am I doing everything I can to be a friend to my neighbor?'

"In closing, I have one more thing to say. The paint is not even dry on the plaza sign, but I think already it needs to be changed. Paul is having a new sign built and it will be erected soon. It shall say, never to be changed, 'Merle Anderson's Friendship Plaza.'"

Chapter 13

The people instantly broke into loud applause. Many turned to face where Merle was standing. Some in the crowd called out, "Speech! Speech, Merle! Speech." Then everyone was gleefully calling his name.

Merle shrugged his shoulders, not wanting to have any part of any speech when suddenly Larry Price took him by the arm and started him toward the front. "You'd better tell them something," Larry said. "They won't let you out of here without some kinda words."

Merle walked slowly through the crowd, shaking hands and receiving pats on the back from those near the aisle. As he approached the front, Merle walked into the arms and hugs of his family. Moving away, Merle had to stop as Walt, Bob and Bill stood in his path. Walt wrapped his arms around Merle and patted him on the back as he said, "We didn't realize what was happening, Merle. Please forgive us. We didn't know." Merle didn't say anything, just smiled and rubbed the top of Bob's head as he walked on through toward the speakers' platform.

After shaking hands with the mayor and receiving his thanks, Merle walked to the podium. As Merle stood at the podium looking out over the crowded plaza, the people continued to stand and applaud. Merle had no idea what he would say. Maybe if they kept standing and applauding he wouldn't have to say anything. No such luck! The people started returning to their seats and the plaza suddenly became very still. Now they sat waiting for his first words.

"Friends!" he managed to say in a shaky voice. "I'm not an educated man. I hope you don't expect a flowery talk, like those that preceded me. All I know to talk about is how I feel and I feel very humble at this moment." Several minutes passed before he continued.

"Thirty-one years ago I brought my young wife and baby sons to your community. I was accepted. They were accepted. It happened almost overnight. This community extended its hand of friendship and we were one of you. I thank you for that. We worked here. We played here and we worshipped here. These are the things that made it a hometown.

"Many were the times we pulled together as a community. Remember the big snow of '63 and the flood of '69? We survived those with little difficulty because we all worked together.

"When I really found out how much you people

meant to me was at the funeral of my wife, Em. The church was full. Many of you that was there are in our audience today. You came to that funeral because you loved Em and her family. The tears you shed were not tears of sympathy, but tears of your loss. You had lost a good friend, one that only a long period of time could replace.

"You see, this is my town. This is our town. That is why I've committed all of my resources to you and our community. My need for money is small, but my need for friends is great. So, thank all of you for being my friends. Thank you."

The crowd in the plaza was dispersing. Five men stood in one corner in deep conversation. Walt was speaking, "You know, guys, what was said here today sure opened my eyes. The things that Simon said sure hit home. I don't believe that I've eaten a half dozen meals at home since we came into this money. We're either eating out, going some place or shopping."

"I know," Bill replied. "We've done the same thing. Plus we've been to Alaska, Florida, and New York. And I'll tell you another thing. I'm miserable until I get back home. Does the money make you happy, Bob?"

"No, it hasn't," Bob replied. "The happiest times of my life were before I ever saw that money."

"Well!" Walt said. "What should we do about it?"

The men walked up the sidewalk toward their vehicles. "I sent all the women home with Carol,"

Paul said. "We're having a get-together with some of our college friends this evening. Can you come up, Merle?"

"No, I don't believe so, Paul," Merle replied. "I can't see too well at night anymore. Besides, your traffic is so bad that it kinda scares me. Besides, you young people need your time to re-hash old times, not to babysit me. By the way, is that true what you said Simon," Merle asked, "about moving back?"

"Yes, it is, Dad. Penny and I have had our fill of D.C. Penny and the girls are going to stay here with Paul and Carol. I'm going back and wrap things up. I should be back about the middle of next month. Penny will be looking for a place to live here in Porterville. We'd like to get settled before school starts."

They arrived at the new, old pickup. "I'll ride with Dad," Peter said. "At least then we will have a few moments to visit before I have to leave." As Merle and Peter were driving down Main, Peter said, "This old truck hasn't aged a day. Looks just like it did when I was a kid."

"I know," Merle replied. "Walt had it completely redone for me. It even drives like new. Peter, do you really have to go back so soon?" Merle asked.

"Yes, Dad, I do. I've got many things to do to get ready for the fall and winter schedule at the Culture Center, but Emily and I will be here next month for the wedding and to be with you."

"Ya know, Son," Merle began, "the best gift that I've ever had was to have you and Simon here with me today. I don't believe anything could ever top this."

Merle pulled the pickup into the parking lot of the Village Cafe. Simon and Paul were standing outside visiting, waiting for them to arrive. The four men walked in and took their seats at Merle's favorite table. Linda hustled over with a tray of water and the coffee pot. After pouring coffee for the men, she looked at Merle. With a smile on her face, she commented, "You old duffer. All this time I've been feeling sorry for you. I even agreed to marry you out of sympathy. Now I'll just marry you for your money." She was chuckling as she walked away.

"What was that all about?" Peter asked.

"Oh, she's just joking," Merle replied. "I'm too old to need a lover, just a friend." Chuckling, Merle continued, "This is a long standing joke between the two of us."

"Not to change the subject about your love life," Simon exclaimed, "but do you think that we could walk over that orchard property in the next day or two? I want to have a home built there as soon as possible."

"Sure, Son," Merle replied. "How about Monday morning? That'll give you a day to rest up from your long trip and busy weekend."

"That's fine, Dad. I'll just meet you here at your coffee break time and we can ride out there together."

Just then five men approached their table. Walt, Bob, Bill, Wayne and Cliff all stood in a semi-circle around the table. All were smiling, but with serious looks on their faces. "Hi, guys," Merle said. "Drag up some chairs. We've had this many crowded around this thing before."

Each of the men fetched a chair from one of the nearby tables while Merle and the others scooted around theirs to make room. After the men were all seated and the coffee was poured, Walt exclaimed, "Simon, Peter. Damn it's good to see you guys. I know Dad here is happy."

"Yes," Simon answered, "it's sure good to be home."

Peter nodded agreement to that statement, "Me too," he said.

The men's conversation went from D.C. to 'Frisco, to Porterville and back again. Each telling of what had been happening over the last five or six years. As the others drew silent, Bill spoke. "Merle, after the ceremony this afternoon we have been taking a hard look at ourselves. To tell the truth, we really don't like what we see. Oh, we appreciate what you've done for us, but we never used it in the right way to make us happy. Fact is, we don't know what happiness is anymore. You tell 'em, Walt."

Walt carried on their plans by saying, "Paul, Simon, we want to do like Merle did. We want to turn our money over to you. Give us just a little to get by on and use the rest to improve the lives of our people and community."

Merle put his hand on Walt's shoulder as he said,

"I'm glad you fellows are doing this. Maybe we can all be best friends again."

"We've always been best friends, Merle. We just kinda forgot for a while."

Finally, Paul said, "Well, fellows, we're going to have to break up this little get together if Simon and I are going to get Emily and Peter to the airport on time. The men all rose and shook hands around the table.

Simon spoke, "I think there'll be a lot of these meetings from now on." They all nodded their heads in agreement.

"I'm glad you're moving back. We need a good lawyer in this town," Bob responded.

As the men began leaving, Merle held back. Looking at Linda with a smile he said, "Say, Linda do you suppose I can charge this until I get my Social Security Check?"

"Get out of here, you old goat!" she laughed. "From now on you're paying double."

Merle climbed into the pickup and gave Gus an affectionate hug. "This is one of the best days of my life, Gus. The very best!" Merle then headed down Main Street, again turning left on Ninth, not knowing why, but again finding himself in the lot of the Burgerville Drive-in.

He pulled in under the sagging canopy. Leaning back in the seat again, he started thinking about all of the events of the day. "A good day, Em," he said aloud. "A very good day. Sure wish you could have been here, Em. You'd have been really proud of your sons."

"I am proud of my sons," came a reply from nowhere. "I'm proud of my sons, and Merle, I'm proud of you. But don't you think it's about time to let me go and look forward to the rest of your life. You can't change the past. Let it go."

Again Merle looked at the far side of the pickup. Again nobody was there, except for Gus. "You're right, Em," he said as he started the truck. "You've always been right." Backing up the truck and heading for the street, Merle drove off into the night.

At that same moment, thirty thousand feet over southern Oregon, Peter and Emily were discussing the day's events. They were laughing about Jack Dunn changing his stripes, about the plaza, the crowd, and the talks that Simon and Dad had made. "You have a wonderful family, Peter," Emily said. "They seem so honest and sincere about human values and life. I think we're going to be very happy."

"I sure hope so Emily. I know I'm going to try very hard."

They sat there thinking in silence for several minutes, then Emily looked at Peter with a worried look on her face. "Peter," she said, "I have an uneasy feeling. I feel that something is not right with your dad."

"What do you mean by that?" Peter exclaimed.

"I don't know," she replied. "But when he gave me that hug in the plaza his hands and his face were so cold. When his cheek touched mine it was cold too, and you know it was a pretty warm day." Peter didn't reply. He just sat there thinking back.

After a short while, Peter responded, "You could be right, now that I think of it. His hands did seem sort of cold. You think he might have a heart or circulation problem?"

"I don't know Peter, but I think you need to go right back. I think you need to get back there as soon as possible."

Peter thought for a few moments of things he had to do, then replied, "I think I will, honey. If I can get Tom to come in tomorrow, I'll get him lined out on what needs to be done and fly back early Monday morning. I think you're right. He needs to see a doctor." What started out to be a happy, carefree flight was now just a means of getting there, for a very concerned couple.

Chapter 14

Merle walked into the coffee shop. Sunday mornings were always the busiest with people eating on their way to church. Merle walked to his table and found it full of his friends. They were all there: Walt, Bob, Bill, Les, Wayne and John. And there was one extra, a new comer to their group—Bill Moore. There was one empty chair. Walt slid the chair back. "We saved this one for you, Merle," he said.

As Merle seated himself and slid his chair into place, Bob said, "If you sit with us, you'll have to buy. We're not going to let you out of this world with one cent in your pocket." They all laughed at that.

"You mean to tell me that you'd take a man's last dime?" Merle chuckled. "I guess you would."

The talk flowed easily around the table. The talk was of the upcoming hunting season and the gripe of the price of deer tags. Bob started talking about the completion date for the youth center, when Merle interrupted. "Please, Bob!" he said. "Our talks at this table have never been serious. Let's don't talk business. Let's just talk about fun things like we used to. We can always talk about things like that at other times in other places. This is our fun place, remember?"

"Sorry," Bob replied. "I'm just so happy about doing something good that I forgot."

"I'm sorry," Merle answered. "I had no right to say that. Maybe we should all quit living in the past. Really, our future is now—what we do today and tomorrow, this week and next. That's our future. Let's enjoy it." There was silence around the table. They didn't know what to say, not believing they'd heard right. Was this Merle talking?

"That's a good idea," Bill said. "A damn good idea."

"Fishing is starting to pick up down on the river," Walt said. "You think next week we oughta go down and give it a try?"

"You guys go ahead," Merle said. "I'll be with Simon the next couple of days, so I'd better not. Walt, you go ahead and take my boat. I'm sure some of these guys will help fill it up." Walt, Bob and Bill sat discussing the fishing trip and telling about how many more fish they'll catch without Merle running the boat.

Wayne turned to Bill Moore and said, "Bill, how about you going with Cliff and me? We'll show these three losers how to fish."

Bill chuckled, "I was hoping for an invitation, me being an outsider and all."

Walt commented on that, "To be an outsider of

this group you'd have to be way out. Welcome to our group of nit-wits!"

Bill Moore wrapped both hands around his cup. "Ya know, fellows, until yesterday I never knew what friendship was all about. But I do know that I want to be one of you. What I guess I'm trying to say is, I want to be a friend, too."

The next morning, Simon sat at his dad's favorite table. He was a little early because he hadn't realized what a short time it took to get here from Spring City. Linda brought his coffee and commented, "You're a little early. Merle won't be here for another twenty or thirty minutes."

"I know," Simon replied. "I kinda miscalculated my time. Oh well, he'll be along shortly."

"That dad of yours is quite a person," she replied. "He sure brightens up the day around here."

"He's always been that way," Simon said. "He never knew a stranger and everyone's a friend. That's been his philosophy his whole lifetime. It has been a pleasure growing up with him as my dad and teacher."

"I bet it was," she said as she moved away to wait on another customer.

Simon took a note pad from his inside coat pocket. As he sipped his coffee, he started noting the events that had happened. These were the notes he'd use to make his report to Washington.

Walt was walking to the familiar table, but stopped as he noticed someone else was already there. Walt could not recognize Simon, with his head down making notes so he sat himself at another table. Linda came hurriedly to his table with the coffee pot. "Morning, Walt," she said. "Merle hasn't got here yet, but his son is at the other table." Walt turned to look just as Simon glanced up from his notes. "Hi, Walt," Simon said. "Come and join me. Dad should be here any time."

Walt picked up his cup and moved opposite Simon. "This is the day you and Merle are going to walk over the orchard property, isn't it? That is a beautiful piece of property. Sure will make a nice home site."

"Yes, I know," Simon said. "Paul is going to work with Penny. They're going to try to have it almost built by the time I get back from D.C."

"Wonder what's keeping Merle?" Walt asked. "He normally gets here before I do."

"It was a pretty busy day Saturday. He's probably still trying to recuperate."

"Maybe so," Walt exclaimed, "but he's the one person who's always on time."

"Yes, but it's still only five 'til nine. Don't worry. He'll be here," Simon replied.

Bob and Bill came in and took their chairs. "Hi, Simon," Bob said. "Where's the old man?"

"Hasn't made it yet," Simon answered. "Should be here in a minute or two."

The four men sat around the table discussing different programs that they might be interested in funding with their money and the minutes slipped slowly by. "Quarter after," Walt said. "That old truck musta broke down."

"Could be," Bill said. "If he's not here in five minutes, we'd better go look for him. It isn't like him to be late."

Walt was looking toward the door when Peter entered. "There's Peter," Walt said. "I thought he went back home."

Simon instantly turned his head. It was Peter approaching the table with a concerned look on his face. "Hi, Peter," Simon said, with a big smile. "What brings you back so soon?"

"Where's Dad?" Peter asked.

"He hasn't got here yet," Simon replied. "What's the matter?"

"I don't know, Simon, but I do know something is not right."

"How's that?" Walt asked.

Peter proceeded to tell them about the conversation on the flight home, about noticing Dad's cold hands and face, and how they had both gotten the feeling at the same time that something was not right. The five men sat at the table in silence for a few moments. All of them had the same feeling now. A feeling that something was not well with Merle.

Simon stood up. "Let's run out there, Peter. He might be sick or something. I think we've waited long enough."

"We'll follow along behind," Walt said. "If

anything is wrong, we want to know. We want to help."

"That's fine with me," Simon replied. "If he is sick there's no one who'll make him well faster than you three."

Turning from the highway onto the lane, Peter remarked, "There's the pickup. He must be here." Simon brought the car to a sliding stop. The two men got out hurriedly and were walking to the door as Walt, Bob and Bill pulled up and also got out.

"I hope he just slept in," Walt said.

"Me too," Simon replied. "It is not like him to do that, but I hope so."

Simon walked to the front door and knocked firmly. He waited for a response, knocked again and when there was still no response, tried to turn the knob. "Locked," he said. "Maybe the back door's open." They all walked to the back of the house, looking in each window as they went. "He doesn't seem to be here," Walt stated. "And he doesn't go any place without that old truck and that dog, Gus."

Reaching the back door, Simon tried the knob. "It's locked too," Simon said. "Walt, look in the woodshed and see if there is something to pry this door open with."

"No!" Peter exclaimed. "The can. The coffee can in the woodshed. There's an extra key there. I'll get it." Peter returned with the key and placed it in the lock, not wanting to find what he thought he'd find. The men entered the house and swiftly went from room to room.

"Not here," Bill said. "I wonder where the heck he could be."

"His secret place," Simon said. "He told me of his secret place."

"You know how to get there?" Peter asked.

"Not really," Simon answered. "But if we look for it hard enough, I suppose it could be found."

"Look at this," Walt said looking at the kitchen table. There on the table were two newspapers, months old. Simon picked up the top paper. The headlines read: "Earthquake Hits Central California Town."

"Well, I'll be," Simon exclaimed. "He told me about this. This was his phone call that saved those peoples' lives. And here, listen to this. 'Three winning tickets in the California Lottery'".

"What's this all about?" Walt asked.

"I'd like to tell you guys, but I'm not. If Dad wants you to know, he can tell you himself. I'm sorry fellows, but I promised him that I'll tell no one," Simon explained.

On the table, back against the wall was a long cardboard tube. Peter picked it up and removed the cap on the end. The other men looked on as Peter pulled the contents out and spread them out on the table. "These are blueprints," Simon said.

"They sure are," replied Bill.

As Peter spread the prints out and held them down with both hands he exclaimed, "These are plans for a log house and a big one too. Look at the dimensions of those rooms and look here. One whole end of the living room is a fireplace."

"Well, I'll be," Simon replied. "The old guy has either built a new home or is going to build one." Turning to the next page of the plans, Simon found a formal piece of paper. He picked it up and read. After a few minutes, he remarked, "This is a construction contract. The completion date was last Saturday. He's probably put this back on the hill someplace. That's where we'll probably find him."

The men left the house and rounded the woodshed to the trail leading up the hillside. They hadn't gone far when Bill said, "If he built it up here, he went a different way than this. This trail hasn't been used for a long time and no way could they get trucks and materials up this way."

"You're right," Simon replied. "If it's up here, there must be another drive some place else. Would one of you guys get in your car and drive back down the road and look for a new drive that's recently been built?"

"I'll go," Bill said. "If there's a way up here I'll find it."

"Thanks," Simon said. "We'll go on up the trail. If it's on this property, we'll find it. Besides, the pickup is at the house. He must be at the new place or somewhere in between."

The four men continued on up the trail, looking at everything, not wanting to miss anything. "That old son-of-a-gun," Walt said. "I wondered what he was doing with all his free time. I see him for coffee every morning, but he's never mentioned what he was doing the rest of the time."

"This is a pretty tough climb," Bob said, "for an old man that hasn't done much for a while." The four men stopped for a few minutes while Bob and Walt got their breath back. As they started to move on up the trail, they heard, "Beep. Beep. Beep." "That's Bill's Jeep horn," Walt said. "He must have found the place already.

They quickened their steps and as they rounded the curve that overlooked the orchard, there it sat. Peter, leading the way, stopped in his tracks. "Why, that is the most beautiful log home I have ever seen. And look how big it is."

Bill, standing in front of his Jeep, was waving and waving. They acknowledged his wave and walked out across the meadow. "I'll bet Dad's up there some-place," Simon said.

"Ya," Bob replied. "He knew if he didn't show up we'd come looking for him. I'll bet that's it, Simon. He's up there watching us, probably grinning from ear to ear."

As the men approached Bill and the Jeep, Simon asked, "Did you see him yet?"

"Nope. Haven't looked. I figure he's here. Probably sitting in there chuckling at us right now."

"I hope so," Peter replied. "I hope this uneasy feel-ing I have will just go away."

The men walked up the steps to the big covered

front porch. "Look at the workmanship," Walt said. "Whoever built this knew what he was doing. It's beautiful."

As they reached the top of the steps, Bob turned and looked out over the valley. "Look at that view. What a place to sit in a rocking chair and retire." They all turned and looked back at the sloping meadow, the tall fir trees and the unobscured view of the mountains across the valley. None of them spoke. They just stood and absorbed the beauty that lay before them.

Simon turned toward the door feeling a little sick inside. This was his land. "Dad gave it to me," he said to himself. "Now I wonder where I can build mine." He wouldn't have long to wonder. There, taped on the window of the front door was an envelope. Pulling it off and turning it over in his hand, he saw written "SIMON." Opening the unsealed envelope and taking out the paper enclosed, he started reading aloud.

"Simon, I knew you'd come back and make your home here someday, but I had no idea it would be so soon. My idea was to have it ready when you did come. This is not a gift. I financed it at the First State Bank and planned on making payments for it from the money I set aside for you. I hope you and Penny will like it. And don't feel badly of me for doing this on my own. Love, Dad."

Chapter 15

Simon slowly turned the knob. "Not locked," he said. Simon eased the large door open, "Dad? Dad, are you here?" There was no response. "Dad, where are you?"

"Doesn't seem to be here," Bob said.

The five men fanned out, going from room to room. "Look at the size of this place," Bob spoke to Walt. "Bet this cost a pretty penny."

"Ya," Walt replied. "Did you see the size of that fireplace? Covered one whole wall." The men left no doors unopened as they searched the house.

Peter was the last to arrive back in the large living room. "There's a big two car garage out back," he said. "But he's not there either. I don't know where he could be. Simon, try to remember the secret place. How'd he say he found it?"

Simon told them the story as his father had told him; about the waterfall, the cave, the tunnel, then the valley. "I know where that waterfall is," Walt responded. "I've hunted with Merle up there. But I never saw no cave."

"You lead the way," Simon said. "We've got to find

it." Walt led off with a hurried pace, heading back to the trail that they'd come up. Reaching the trail, they turned and went single file up the mountain. The trail steepened and the three older men started falling behind. They didn't have the strength to stay up with the younger men.

Simon and Peter went on ahead and were standing beside the waterfall looking in all directions as the three older men arrived. "Yep, this is it," Walt said. "This is the only waterfall that I can remember." The men stood in place, turning slowly, trying not to miss anything. With each revolution they came up with nothing.

"There's no cave here," Bill said. "Unless it's behind some brush. Let's fan out and look it over good." For over an hour they searched the rock wall. One by one each returned to the place where he had started.

"There must be another waterfall in another canyon," Peter exclaimed.

"Well, I'm going down and get John Lock," Walt replied. "He sold this land to your dad. He knows every inch of this property."

"Good idea," Simon said. "But I'm going to go. You're too old to be climbing up and down this mountain. You guys stick close by. I'll be back as soon as I can." Simon turned and trotted down the trail. "John Lock," he said. "Why didn't I think of that?"

Simon pulled the car into John's driveway, stopped, got out and headed for the front door. John stood up and looked over his raspberry vines. He had been stooped over picking a pail of tomatoes when the car pulled up. "Is there something you want, Mister?" John said.

Simon stopped and turned toward the voice. All he could see was John's head. "Hi, John. I need your help."

"Who're you?" John asked. "My eyes aren't so good no more."

"I'm Simon Anderson," was the reply. "Do you remember me?"

"Yes, Simon. How ya been? What kinda help do ya need?"

"John," Simon said, "I can't find Dad. Have you seen him at all?"

"Nope, not since that thing downtown. And then I didn't get to talk to him." John came around the row of berries and leaned on the fence. "Where all did ya look, Simon?" Simon proceeded to tell John everything since he arrived that morning.

"Well," John replied, "there's only one cave I know of and it's up a cliff, just left of that waterfall probably fifty or sixty feet up on that cliff. It's really not a cave, just kinda a washout in the cliff. Hell, Simon, let me tell Nora where I'm a goin' and I'll show ya."

"I sure would appreciate it, John, if you would."

John quietly opened the bedroom door. There a frail Nora lay. Her only movement was the rise and fall of her chest from the slow and shallow breaths she labored to draw. John went to his knees beside the bed and took her hand into his. "Hi, Honey. How you feeling today?" he asked softly.

Nora turned her head slightly to look at John. There was no other response. "I'm going to be gone a little while. Merle's lost. I'm going to help the boys find him." Again there was no response or answer, but John knew there wouldn't be.

"They think he's up in that valley, you know, the one I told you about. I'll be back just as soon as I can, and Alice will be here in a few minutes." As John started to get up, he felt a very light squeeze of his hand. John stood there a few moments holding her hand in his, looking into her face. He laid her hand gently beside her. "I said that I'll hurry back, Honey, I promise. I'll hurry right back." As John walked to the door, Nora's eyes slowly followed, then he was gone. With her eyes still open, she could see nothing, nothing at all.

Another car came into the drive as John was opening the door to Simon's car. It stopped and an older plump lady in a starched white dress got out. "Hi, Alice," John said.

"Hi," came the reply. "How's our girl today?"

"'Bout the same," he answered. "Although when I told her I was going to the mountain, she squeezed my hand. Anyway, I think she did. I'll be gone a little while. Gonna help Simon find Merle. See ya later."

"Okay, John. I'll stay til you get back."

"Is your wife sick or something, John?" Simon asked.

"She's pretty bad," came a reply. "Been expecting her to leave us the last month or two."

"Sorry," Simon said. "Maybe you shouldn't leave?"

"No!" John said. "Alice will stay til I get back. Nora really doesn't know if I'm here or not."

A short time later Simon and a wheezing old man came walking up to the group. "Took you longer than I thought," Peter said.

John, puffing hard, with a wheeze in his voice said, "Been here sooner, if I hadn't smoked all them cigarettes over the years. Simon had to wait for me three or four times."

"Where's it at?" Simon asked John, looking up scanning the face of the cliff.

"Thar she is. See? Ya can just see the very top of it from here."

"Yah! I see it," Walt replied. "How in the heck are we going to get up there?"

John looked back down the trail. "See that little game trail? Follow it. It should take you right up there."

"You sit here and rest," Simon said. "We'll go up and have a look." Simon led the way. Single file the men climbed the trail that came out on the ledge. "He never told me about this part," Simon said. "We'd never have found this without John's help."

The men rounded the large boulder and stood looking at the mouth of the large washout. Slowly, they walked to the entrance. "This must be the place," Simon said. "There's where he had a fire."

"Yah," Walt said. "You can see the whole inside and he's sure not here."

"Wait a minute. He said something about a smaller cave in one corner. Over there. That must be it over there," Simon seemed to be talking to himself as he hurriedly walked across the soft sand. Simon came to the entrance of the little cave.

"See anything?" Peter asked.

"No, it's too dark. I don't suppose anyone has a flashlight?" Simon asked.

"Here, I do," Bob replied. "Not much of a light, just a pen light on my key chain. Want me to go first?" he asked.

"No!" Simon replied. "Let me use your light. I'd like to go first."

"OK, here it is, Simon. You have to hold the button down with your thumb, otherwise it won't stay on."

Taking the light from Bob, Simon led the way, each man falling in behind, putting his hand on the one in front for guidance. "Watch your heads," Simon said. "This roof's pretty low."

The five men emerged from the cave's mouth into the sunlight. They stood there in awe! They were looking at the most beautiful place they'd ever seen. "Do you believe this place?" Bill asked.

"Never seen anything like it," Bob replied. "If I didn't know better, I'd swear that I'm standing in the path to heaven."

Simon and Peter were speechless. In all their travels throughout the world, neither had seen or felt the serenity that they were now feeling in this place. "Dad was right," Simon said to Peter. "He said it was the most beautiful place he'd ever seen. There's the trail. That must be the trail he spoke of."

The five men walked slowly down the stone lined trail. Each one was hypnotized by the beauty of the valley laying before them. As they rounded a large tree alongside the trail, Simon spoke in a soft voice, "There it is. There's the pool and the waterfall."

"Why are ya whispering?"

"I don't know," Simon replied.

"You're not going to scare that pool," Bill said. "It's not going to get up and run away."

"I know," Simon replied, "but don't you feel like you're in a special place? A place where you wouldn't want to disturb a thing."

"You mean, kinda like a church or something?"

"Yes, I guess that's what I'm trying to say," Simon said. "Come on. Let's go on down."

The men moved slowly on down the trail and were soon looking into the blue water of the deep pool. "Hi, fellows," came Merle's voice from behind. All turned abruptly and saw Merle sitting on a stone bench with Gus sleeping with his head on Merle's leg.

"Dad!" Simon said. "We've been worried sick about you. Why didn't you meet me at the cafe?"

"I couldn't," Merle replied. "I tried but I couldn't."

Merle handed a rolled up paper to Peter.

"What's this?" Peter exclaimed.

"Read the second article on page two," Merle answered.

Peter took the paper from Merle's outstretched hand, turned the page and began to read to himself, then shortly handed the paper to Simon. "You knew, Peter, didn't you?" questioned Merle.

Peter responded in a soft, shaky voice, "I suspected something was wrong, but I didn't know what."

"That's why you came back, isn't it?"

"Yes it is, Dad. I just couldn't stay away."

"I know your mother told you. I don't know how she did, but I know she found a way."

"What are you talking about?" Bob asked. "None of this makes sense to me."

Simon handed the article to Bob. Bob, Bill and Walt crowded together and read the article at the same time. Walt finished the article before the other two and said, "That said you died. What the h—(no word would come)."

"There's no swearing in this place Walt. Remember that."

Walt's voice came back. "If that's so," he said, "how come you're talking to us? Why are we here?"

Merle replied, "When I knew for sure that Peter suspected, I couldn't tell you over there. You wouldn't believe me, but in this place we can see the future and tell no lies. Remember that as we visit today."

"Dad," Simon said with tears running down his cheeks, "how long? How long have you been here?"

"Since the first day I came into this valley and sat on this bench. This bench is the key that unlocks the veil. Now each of you find a place to sit and let's have a good visit." The five men all seated themselves facing Merle.

"Simon," Merle asked, "how do you like your new house?"

"It's beautiful! How did you know the kind of house Penny and I have been dreaming about?"

"That's the whole secret," Simon. "If you hadn't dreamed, I'd never have known."

"Well, I'll be!" Bob said. "You knew everything us three guys were planning before we ever picked up those checks, didn't ya?"

"Sure did," Merle replied. "There's been no secrets for the last eight months."

"You knew all about Jack Dunn then?" Simon asked.

"Yes, I gave him a little help on that one. Turned out pretty good, didn't it?"

"I wondered how a skunk like that could change his stripes," Simon said.

Walt looked at Merle with concern on his face. "Merle," he said. "We're all in this valley. Does that mean we're all dead too?"

"No, Walter, only if you sit on this bench. You can come here as often as you wish. You can find answers to most things here just by looking into the pool of knowledge. This is my place. This is my bench. Everyone will have their place and their bench some- where at some time."

There was silence in the group of men now. All were looking down trying in their minds to digest what they'd just heard. A father and friend was go- ing to leave them soon and there wasn't a thing they could do about it.

Finally, Merle broke the silence. "I want you to look over there," pointing to the far mountain. The men rose and turned toward the mountains.

"What? I don't see nothing," Bill said.

"There. See that eagle?" Merle replied.

"Oh, yes. The one flying back and forth."

"That's her," Merle said. "She's been looking for her mate for a long time."

"You think she'll ever find him?" Walt asked.

"I think she will," Merle replied. "Very soon, I think." Suddenly there was an eagle cry overhead. A large eagle was circling over where the men stood. They all stood there watching as the big bird dipped its wings and flew across the canyon to meet the awaiting bird. After circling each other a few times, they seemed to glide down the canyon under the afternoon sun. Following close behind them was a much smaller bird, darting from side to side.

Simon spoke in a soft voice, "Goodbye, Dad. Bye, Gus."

"Why'd you say that, Simon?" Walt asked.

"I don't know," Simon said. "It just came out."

All the men turned slowly to look back at Merle, not knowing what they'd find. Merle sat there with a big smile on his face. "Well, how'd you like it? How do you like my place?"

"But . . . but, I thought when that eagle flew away, that you'd left us," Peter said.

"Gosh, no!" Merle replied. "That was old John Lock. He's known of this place years before me."

"But what about the paper?" Peter asked.

"Oh, heck! That's a Monday paper and they don't amount to much. And besides, look at the date— March 17, 2021. You see, I'll be around a long time yet. But I do ask you all to keep this place and happenings a secret.

"I don't know why not," Bill replied. "Nobody would believe us anyway."

Simon looked at his dad and asked, "You could have left, couldn't you?" Merle nodded his head in a yes motion. "I know you really miss Mom. What made you decide to stay?"

"Well, let me see!" was Merle's response. "The new old truck's not worn out yet. I've got my family and friends back. Old Gus still gets around pretty good and I've got a date with Linda next Saturday night."

The six men walked up the trail, laughing, joking and thinking of the future. As they approached the entrance, they saw a frail old man sitting on a fallen log, leaning back against a large rock with his chin resting on his chest. "Is that John?" Walt asked.

"Yes," came Merle's reply. "We both knew his time was short. He just needed a reason to get back up here. You guys gave him that reason. We'd better pick up what's left of him and take him to the other side," Merle said.

Simon gently picked John up and followed Peter into the cave entrance. The four older men turned to look out over the valley one more time. The two eagles still circled in the distance in and out of the sun's golden rays.

Merle turned his head slightly and spoke to the others. "As we pass from today into tomorrow, we shall arrive there on the wings of an eagle."

Three of the men turned toward the entrance. Merle stood there alone looking at a lonely eagle flying to and fro. In a low voice that only he could hear, he said, "I'm sorry, Em. Maybe next time. Yes, maybe next time."

About The Author

Bob Glenn was born in a small town in Kansas, sixty-four years ago.

In 1934, due to the Depression and the dust, he migrated to California like so many others at that time. Bob's early youth was spent going from town to town, from school to school, following his family wherever there might be work.

His biggest break in life came in 1943 when his family moved to Cottage Grove, Oregon. He finally had a town he could call home. He graduated from Cottage Grove High School in 1949, and he has lived, played and worshipped in Cottage Grove most of his adult life.

Bob spent four years serving in the Navy and five years as a zone manager for the Dr. Pepper Co. The rest of the time he worked in the trucking industry as a driver, manager, and owner until his retirement in 1993.

As a poet—always. As a writer—never . . . until now. We hope you enjoy reading this story as much as Bob has enjoyed writing it.